# MARRY ME

SUSAN SCOTT SHELLEY

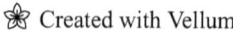 Created with Vellum

# CHAPTER ONE

## DAMON

The ominous gray sky echoed the mutinous feeling spiraling through Damon Kallis's blood. He guided his SUV through streets covered with snow thanks to a mid-January storm and replayed the conversation with his future in-laws over and over in his head.

Beside him, his fiancée Emily stared out the window. She hadn't said a word since they'd left her parents' home half an hour earlier. For her to be this quiet for this long wasn't normal. Neither was the stiffness in her posture or the wringing of her hands.

The cheerful lunch with her family had turned into a sneak attack. The way they had waylaid he and Emily, launching into a full-on guilt trip and strong encouragement to get married at the family's church and have the reception in the ballroom at their upscale country club, despite the wait-list of three years, had soured his stomach.

"You're quiet." Emily's voice pierced the silence.

"Your parents gave us a lot to think about."

Wanting to make a good impression had won out over the desire to tell them to leave the decisions to him and his new fiancée. But he regretted that he and Emily hadn't previously discussed wants and wishes for their big day prior to setting foot inside her parents' home.

Since their engagement at Christmas, his employees had teased them both about their newly-engaged glow. Though, neither of he nor Emily were smiling or glowing right now.

He'd left their home with a throbbing head and a desire for a stiff drink, both of which increased with Emily's promise to her parents that they'd think about the venue. That he and Emily had only been together for a short period of time didn't matter, no way did he want to wait another three whole years to get married.

They needed to talk, but first, they needed to get through dinner with his friends and sister. A dinner they were already running late to, thanks to the winter misery holding Western New York in a death grip.

Glaring at the thick snowflakes falling at a steady pace, he parked outside his sister's house and then exited his SUV. A slick street made walking treacherous. He hurried to the vehicle's other side to take his fiancée's hand as she climbed out of the car's warmth.

"Careful. The ground is slippery."

"Thanks for the warning." As Emily stepped out of the car, her voice and expression echoed the weariness Damon felt all the way to his core.

Holding hands, they began slow, careful steps up the snow-covered path from the street to the house.

A gust of wind slapped icy air against his skin, but also carried the scent of Emily's perfume. Every time he looked at his dark-haired, dark-eyed dream come true, warmth filled his soul. Emily had returned a happiness to him that he'd thought he'd never find again. Her love made every single day better.

Even days that were miserably stressful.

As they approached the door, Damon squeezed Emily's hand. He could smell the chocolate cake they'd picked up for dessert as the scent wafted from the box she carried.

When they reached the door, he paused with his finger over the doorbell. Raised voices carried through from the other side, the words sharp and tight.

Emily grabbed his arm. "Sounds like they're fighting. Maybe we should come back later."

The door swung open before he could make a decision to stay or go. Hunter, his best friend and his sister Kira's fiancé, waved them inside. "I saw you walking up the path."

Still, Emily hesitated in the threshold. "We can do dinner another night if this isn't a good time."

Hunter shook his head, and his sandy brown hair flopped against his forehead in messy strands. Lines of stress fanned out around his eyes and mouth. "I don't see it getting better, so just come in."

Damon stepped inside. He took one look at his sister's tear-streaked face, and the urge to put something through a wall crashed down faster and harder than an avalanche. "What happened?"

Kira brushed her hands over her cheeks and then wrapped her arms around herself. Her cheeks were too pale against her brown hair and red sweater. "We just found out that we have to find a new wedding venue. There was a fire at the catering hall this afternoon."

"How bad?" Damon crossed to her, his gut tightening. "Was anyone hurt?"

"No, thank goodness," Kira said, "but there's so much damage that they're not even sure if they can reopen by the summer, let alone within two months."

"And you gave them a hefty deposit—"

"They returned it, so no worries there," Hunter cut in. He massaged his temples and sighed. "But after all the planning we did, we can't change the date now. We have a better chance of winning the lottery than finding a new reception venue in less than two months. Every place I could think of is already booked."

"There's got to be a solution," Emily soothed as she set the bakery box down. "We'll help you think of something."

The doorbell rang, and Hunter shuffled past Damon to open the door.

Aidan and Skye came in, along with a blast of cold air, and their dog Chance. Their expressions were just as tension-filled as Hunter and Kira's. Damon frowned. More wedding drama? Man, eloping was starting to sound pretty damned good.

Skye stalked past Damon and yanked off her hat,

scarf, and coat. Aidan's troubled eyes met Damon's gaze, and his normally easy-going friend shrugged out of his coat, shoulders slumped like he carried the world's weight and had decided it was too much to bear. Chance darted between Skye and Aidan, rubbing his head against their legs before settling beside Aidan.

He needed some intel if he was going to help. Damon leaned close to his other best friend. "What's going on?"

Aidan opened his mouth, but before he could say a word, Skye spun around. The delicate blonde had the light of battle in her brown eyes. "You know how Aidan and I haven't really made any wedding plans yet? Well, that's been driving my mom crazy. So she took it upon herself to select a date and booked us a church, reception site, and florist back home. She sprung all of that on me this morning. I've been on the phone for *hours* today. It took forever to cancel everything. I need a drink." She strode toward the open bottle of wine and glasses on the coffee table.

Damon caught the flash of hurt on Aidan's face before it slipped away and his gut clenched. Aidan and Skye had been engaged since Labor Day, nearly five months now. A few times over the months since that day, Aidan had voiced his concern to Damon and Hunter that he wasn't sure why Skye kept putting off the planning and how he feared that maybe she didn't want to get married anymore.

Watching Skye poured a healthy amount of wine and then drained the glass, Damon shared a glance with

Hunter. Could Aidan be right? Was there more than a Momzilla of the Bride going on here?

The tension radiating off of Skye charged the air and silence descended on the room as Damon, Hunter, Emily, and Kira all looked at each other. What could he say? What could any of them do to defuse this?

After a moment, Kira cleared her throat and crossed to Skye and laid a hand on her arm. "Your mom totally overstepped, but I think she was just trying to help."

Skye set down her glass with a loud clink. "I know it. I just…" She shook her head and her features creased as she played with her engagement ring. "I can't do it."

Aidan's posture stiffened. Hurt and surprise twisted his features. His mouth worked open and then closed as he absorbed the words and then his hands clenched into fists at his sides, and he drew in a deep breath. "You don't want to marry me anymore?"

Emily pulled on Damon's arm and then inclined her head toward the kitchen. He knew she was right. They should give Aidan and Skye privacy. But, damn it, he didn't want to leave in case Aidan needed him and Hunter. Still, he backed up toward the kitchen, and Hunter and Kira followed. The layout allowed him a small view of the living room, and although he tried not to, he couldn't drag his gaze away.

Skye turned toward Aidan. Her face softened, and she closed the distance between them. "Of course, I want to marry you."

"Then why do you kept changing the topic every time I bring up making wedding plans?"

A blush rose high in Skye's cheeks. "I've been dragging my feet with making decisions because I don't want to deal with my mom. You know how she is. How she makes me feel. How she always brings up my scars. I know it's not mean-spirited, and that her reminders about using sunscreen and covering the skin are out of love, but she gets so worked up and overprotective and calls so much attention to me. Being the center of attention in front of the two hundred people she wants us to invite is going to be scary and hard enough for me, but with her there on overdrive? I just can't handle that too."

A stab of sympathy throbbed in Damon's chest. Skye bore burn scars on the left side of her body, reminders of the horrible fire she'd survived. She was still self-conscious about the scars, even though she'd come a long way from the first time he'd met her.

Feeling a little embarrassed to be basically eavesdropping on such a private moment, Damon pulled Emily closer, needing her warmth. He murmured, "I wish there were something I could do."

She hugged him tight. "That's why I love you."

In the living room, Aidan took Skye's hands in his. "I saw how your mom acted when we visited them at Thanksgiving and seeing you so stressed out and upset drove me crazy. I tried to shield you the best I could then, and that's not going to stop now. I'll do whatever I can to make us happy. Just tell me what you want."

"I don't want to get married back home."

"Then we won't. We can get married here or anywhere else. We'll plan it all out, get every detail taken care of, and then tell your mom everything is all set. The only thing she and your dad will have left to do is show up that day. And I'll employ whatever resources are needed to ensure she's distracted enough to not go the overprotective, attention-calling mode."

"She's not going to understand why I've changed my mind about a beach wedding back home. Miami isn't special to me since you're not a part of it."

Damon nudged Emily and nodded at Kira and Hunter. It was safe to go back into the room. The tightness in his chest eased at the sight of Aidan and Skye embracing.

Emily squeezed his hand and whispered to him, "I have an idea."

Brow raised, wondering what she meant, he followed her into the living room.

She poured wine into a glass from the open bottle on the counter then handed it to Skye. "A beach wedding could still be nice, if you want it, and not in Miami. There's a hotel I love in Virginia Beach. It's not huge, but it's beautiful, and on a section of the beach that's really private. I've pictured myself getting married there, but if one of you guys wants it, I'll give you the information. March would be kind of off-season for the hotel so Kira and Hunter's wedding date might be available."

Kira's brows shot up. "That's the place you visit every summer, right? I wonder if it would be warm enough there in March to hold something outside."

"I have no idea since I've only been there in the summer." Emily grinned. "But even if it's too cold to hold anything outside, the hotel has an observatory on its top floor. That would be a beautiful setting for a wedding."

Hunter wrapped his arms around Kira and rested his chin on the top of her head. "That sounds good to me."

"Or Skye," Emily turned toward Skye and Aidan. "It's sort of halfway between here and Miami, so your family wouldn't have to travel too far. Maybe you and Aidan could go there, and if you love it, that's a great reason to want to get married there."

Snuggled against Aidan's side, Skye sipped her wine. "What's it called?"

"Here, I'll show you." Emily pulled out her phone and brought up the hotel's site. Pictures of tranquil rooms, the observatory on the top floor that looked out over the ocean, and artfully styled foods moved across the small screen.

What caught Damon's attention most was Emily's smile as she scrolled through the pictures. A smile that had been missing when her parents had discussed their country club.

"I love it." Kira tilted the screen for Hunter to see. "It's perfect."

"It really is. Very peaceful and pretty." Skye nodded. Then, she glanced at Kira, and some of the light in her eyes dimmed. "But Kira and Hunter have the more immediate need. They should call and see if it's available."

Kira swept Skye into a tight hug. "Thank you."

Hunter picked up his phone. He wrapped his other

hand around Kira's shoulder and nodded toward the kitchen. "Let's call now."

As soon as Hunter and Kira walked into the other room, Damon pulled Emily aside. "If you want to get married there, why didn't you say something when we were at your parents' place today? Your family is great, and I respect traditions, but if Virginia Beach is what you want, then that's what we'll do."

"But that's kind of far. And making everyone travel there when most of them live closer to here—"

"Is something that people will understand if they really want you to be happy. And they do. I'm sure no one will mind traveling too much." Damon grasped her hands and then braced himself before adding, "I don't want to wait three years to marry you. But I will if you really want to use the place your family is pushing."

"But what about you?" Emily's gaze searched his face. "Where do you want to get married?"

"All I want is you. The rest is just details. And I'd like these guys to be there," he gestured to the group. "Really. It could be a swamp. A backyard. A ballroom. A hockey rink. I don't care as long as we're married at the end of it."

Tension drained out of Emily's body and she leaned up and kissed his jaw. "Thank you. But I can't call dibs on that hotel now. Not if it ends up working out for Kira and Hunter."

Kira came into the room, holding the phone to her chest, and grinning. "They have our date available. And they can get us a block of hotel rooms too. I'm trying to think of how many we'll need. Damon, do you think twenty rooms will be enough?"

Damon ran through the list of family members, then caught the way Aidan was rubbing Skye's back, and Emily's longing stare at the hotel's site. Maybe there was a way to fix everyone's problems. "I have an idea. Hunter, you wanted both Aidan and me to be your best men. I know I want you and Aidan to do that for me."

Aidan nodded. "I want both of you too."

He looked at his friends, hell, his brothers. They'd done everything together since meeting in boot camp— served together in the Army, followed by working together at his family's company—so why should a wedding be any different? "Why don't all of us get married at the same time?"

"A triple wedding?" Hunter's brows rose, and then he smiled and nodded. "Hell, yeah. That's great."

"It's going to be a lot of the same guests at all three weddings anyway, so it's easier for them to only have to travel to one," Damon spoke fast to head off any doubts. "And this way, planning would be easy. We're never going to make all the families happy, so we might as well make ourselves happy." Especially him, because he could give Emily what she really wanted.

She met his gaze with wide eyes. Surprise and excitement and something else he couldn't name swirled in the brown depths. "That's so soon. We've only been engaged for a few weeks."

Damon's enthusiasm froze. "Too soon?"

"No. Just… I'm not sure how people will feel. We're

not giving them a lot of time. And everyone in my family is going to think I'm pregnant." Emily twisted her engagement ring around and around.

The third time the stones caught the lights in the room, Damon closed his hand over hers. "People are always joking that Hunter and Aidan and I do everything together, and when we explain things, I'm sure your family will understand. We'll have a party when we get back for anyone who can't make it."

Emily wrapped her arms around his waist and squeezed. Her eyes sparkled with her smile, but then the happiness faded, and she twisted to face Kira. "We would be horning in on your wedding day. I don't want to cause any problems or put you on the spot. You guys have been planning for a long time and already have a picture in your heads of how you want the wedding to be. A six-person wedding would be a huge change. Maybe we shouldn't decide this now."

Gaze thoughtful, Kira tapped her finger against the phone and tilted her head to the side, but a small smile grew on her lips.

Hunter ambled toward her. "They say things happen for a reason."

"True." Lips pressed together, she turned toward Skye. "Skye, what do you think?"

"All of us together?" Skye's voice, filled with hope and relief, was as low as a whisper. "I like that idea. A lot. And not just because I'm being a coward. Having you guys involved means that my mom can't try to take over everything again. And all of the attention would be spread out and not so focused on me."

At that, the uncertainty in Kira's gaze shifted to sympathy. "Then let's do it. It would be so much fun to share this with you guys."

Damon nudged his sister's shoulder. As much as he wanted the idea, he didn't want her to end up resenting him. "Are you sure?"

"I'm sure. Hunter's right. Things do happen for a reason. Aidan, you haven't said anything. Is this plan okay with you?"

"It's perfect." Aidan ran one hand down Skye's back, and she pressed a kiss to his cheek. Chance barked and jumped up, placing his front paws on the couple. Laughing, Aidan rubbed the dog's head. "Ask if we can get this guy in on it too."

Limp with relief that the people who mattered so much to him were all in agreement with his crazy idea, Damon grinned. "So, we're really doing this?"

Everyone cheered, and the room filled with excited chatter and loud barking from Chance.

"Guys, quiet. Before we get too excited, let me run it all by the events coordinator. And I think we'll need to at least double the number of hotel rooms." Kira pulled the phone to her ear and strode into the kitchen again.

While she spoke into the phone, the rest of the group waited in silence. Damon exchanged glances with everyone during the collective breath-holding. There still was a hurdle or two to clear. Emily gripped his hand and Skye crossed her fingers.

Finally, Kira returned, and her smile revealed the event's coordinator answer. "We're in."

More cheers filled the room, and Damon high-fived the guys.

"She loved the idea of a triple wedding, and it's fine for Chance to come too," Kira continued. "She's going to email us some questions about colors and theme and menu, and then they'll take care of the decorations, flowers, food, and cake."

"Cake is important." Hunter nodded toward the chocolate cake Emily had brought in. "We should fly down for a weekend and do a tasting."

Kira nodded. "She suggested we do just that, and we can finalize the menu and cake and everything then. Skye and Emily, you guys need wedding dresses. Two months isn't much time."

Emily brushed her hair off her shoulder and leaned against Damon. "I have my grandmother's dress. I need to get it altered and modernized, but I know what I want, and one of my cousins is a seamstress, so I don't see any reason why I won't have it in time."

Skye reached for her wine glass again. "My mom has been sending me tons of photos, but I have no idea what I want. I need to go shopping, but I'm dreading it. I hate hovering salespeople."

Her self-consciousness about her scars had gotten better, but being the center of attention, especially in a public place, was hard for her.

Kira exchanged glances with Emily, and they both

crossed to Skye. "We'll make it fun. Don't worry. It'll be just the three of us."

"And we'll get there first-thing, so we hopefully have the shop to ourselves," Emily added. "Maybe we can even request a private appointment."

Skye tugged on her hair, smoothing the strands over her cheek. "Thanks, guys."

Relief in his gaze and his shoulders relaxed, Aidan clamped his hand on Damon's shoulder. "Great idea, man. Thanks for coming up with it."

The oven timer beeped from the kitchen and Hunter beckoned them toward the room. "Dinner's ready."

After they had eaten, they spent hours crowded around the computer, discussing food and flowers and colors and logistics. Through it all, Damon held Emily's hand. The only problem he could foresee was the conversation he and Emily would have to have with her parents about ditching the family church and country club for a beach hotel a plane ride away. He didn't want problems with his future in-laws, but making Emily happy and sharing the wedding with the people he loved most was more important than potentially ruffling a few feathers. Sharing the celebration was the right decision.

Together, always, was the best way to go.

# CHAPTER TWO

## KIRA

The trouble with a destination wedding was in getting to the destination.

Kira stared out the SUV's window, unable to see much with the swirling flakes, thick clouds, and snow-covered highway all blending into a wall of white. The freak March storm had turned into a full-blown nor'easter, grounding flights and forcing most means of travel to a standstill.

Not at all convenient for her wedding weekend.

If they ever arrived at the destination.

What should have been a ten-hour trip from their Buffalo-area suburb of Holiday, New York to Virginia Beach, Virginia had already stretched into sixteen. And they still had one hundred miles to cover. Playing with her engagement ring, she turned toward Hunter.

Her fiancé's profile was a study in concentration. His brown eyes narrowed at the huge semi that thundered past, showering their car in a blast of snow. For a moment, visibility disappeared completely, and the car shook from the wind buffeting off of the truck.

The car skidded toward the guard rail, and Kira gripped the edge of her seat as her stomach dipped and her heart slammed into her ribcage. Too many slips and slides and near-collisions with other vehicles had turned this trip into a deadly obstacle course. Guilt curled through her fear. If they were in an accident, it would be her fault. Ever since the day they'd agreed on the triple wedding, she'd insisted on driving down to the venue because she hadn't trusted the airline not to lose her wedding dress, and hadn't wanted to chance shipping it to the hotel ahead of time.

Beside her, Hunter swore and spun the steering wheel until the car was once again in the highway lane. Usually calm under stress, he'd been grumbling and glowering for the past several hours. "Idiot driver. He's going to cause an accident."

He grimaced and dropped one hand to his thigh, massaging the muscles.

Sitting for so long wasn't good. Especially not for Hunter. He still suffered nerve pain from bullet wounds he'd sustained while deployed in Afghanistan. And cold weather aggravated his injuries.

"You've been driving for a long time. Why don't we switch, so you can put the seat back and stretch your legs?" She'd packed a battery-operated heating pad and a mini-massager for him.

He glared at the road ahead. "I'm fine."

"Hunter..." She didn't want to fight. Not about this.

Not again. He usually let her help him, but every so often, he pulled his pain inward and tried to soldier on in spite of it, and that drove her crazy.

Brakes screeched, and car horns honked, accompanying the strains of the rock music playing from the speakers. The aggressive tunes weren't helping soothe her at all, but Hunter kept choosing them every time it was his turn to control the music.

The sea of white grew deeper, and they passed more and more abandoned cars on the side of the highway.

"This is crazy. I can't see more than a few feet in front of me." Hunter gripped the wheel tight again and scowled at the falling flakes.

"Maybe we should get off at the next exit."

"It's taken us an hour to drive three miles. At this rate, it'll take four hours before we reach the next exit." He cursed as the car slipped again. "I wish I had my own car. This one sucks."

Kira winced and twisted to peer into the backseat. The garment bags containing her, Skye's, and Emily's dresses and the guys' tuxes lay flat next to the suitcases and the supplies they'd packed for the road trip. Volunteering to help out her friends by taking their dresses and tuxes had been the right thing to do, but the sense of responsibility, especially with all the near-accidents, was as heavy as a six-foot snow drift.

The car's speed decreased until a turtle could have passed them as Hunter followed the flow of traffic. Eventually, they came to a stop.

Minutes passed in tense silence. No sound of sirens,

nothing indicating an accident up ahead, so why weren't they moving?

"I wonder what's going on." Kira found a news station and the radio crackled with a mix of static and words.

Hunter slapped his palm against the rental's dashboard and then raised the volume.

Kira leaned forward, straining to hear the newscaster's words. "...sections of I-95, I-495, and I-64 have been shut down as snow accumulation has reached ten inches in most areas. Law enforcement is reporting several abandoned cars and jackknifed tractor-trailers that have clogged the road, preventing state workers from clearing the snow. The interstate will be closed until six a.m. tomorrow morning, the storm's expected end. Hundreds of vehicles are trapped due to the conditions. Emergency responders are attempting to reach the stranded motorists. Drivers are being asked to remain in their vehicles."

Hunter sat back with a huff. "And now we know why we're not moving."

"But... The rehearsal dinner is tonight."

"Not for us." He pulled his pinging phone from the cup holder. "I got a text from Damon. He and Emily's flight was rerouted, and they had to drive partway. They're stuck in a hotel in Baltimore. So they won't make it tonight either."

Kira dug her phone from her purse. It buzzed with texts from her brother, Emily, and Skye. "That's awful. At least Skye and Aidan arrived safely." They'd flown out a few days earlier. Something she and Hunter should have done. But work had come first, and with the launch of toy factory's much anticipated newest release, neither had felt right about taking off when both of their departments needed them.

"Yeah." Hunter turned the car off and reached for his hat and gloves.

Relieved by the sudden silence, she watched him pull on his winter-wear. "Where are you going?"

"The snow's already piling up. I need to make sure it's not clogging the exhaust pipe. If we don't do that, the car can fill up with carbon monoxide."

"I'll come help."

"No. Stay here. No use in both of us wading through this mess." He left the car. A moment later, he opened the rear door and began pushing the bags. "Where's the snow shovel?"

"It should be there."

"Well, it's not. The only thing here is an extra windshield scraper." He held up the small blue piece of plastic.

"Crap." Kira scrambled into her coat, hat, and gloves. "I pulled out the shovel when I was sliding in the luggage. I didn't see it leaning against the garage door when we left, so I thought you put it back in the car."

"Nope. I didn't see it. There wasn't anything against the door."

"So that bump we hit when we pulled out of the driveway? I'm betting that was the shovel's handle." It had probably fallen into the snowbank at the side of the driveway. They'd left a winter wonderland in Holiday.

"Great." Sarcasm seared the word. He closed the rear door and began kicking the drifts of snow away from the car.

Kira opened her door and sucked in a breath at the cold. She sank into snow that reached the tops of her boots and waded toward Hunter. He winced each time he swung his leg. When he met her gaze, he shook his head. "You should go back inside the car."

"You should let me help you and stop being so stubborn." She knelt in front of the exhaust pipe. There wasn't much snow inside, and she was able to remove it before Hunter finished clearing a space around her.

They'd packed well for their trip. Growing up in an area used to large amounts of annual snowfall, she knew the essentials to keep in a car during the winter just in case a situation like this arose. They had a few bottles of water, a box of nutrition bars, two wool blankets, two flashlights, and the sleeping bag they used on camping trips. And the snacks and beverages they'd brought specifically for the trip.

The most important thing was to remain calm. The authorities knew where they were. She'd send a text to Skye and to Damon. All they needed to do was stay warm enough to get through the night, or until help arrived.

Sweat coated her skin as she helped kick and carry snow from the back of the car. The shovel would have come in handy. As the amount of snow around the car decreased, her guilt, over both not making sure the shovel had been replaced, and over driving in the first place, piled high and sunk her spirits faster than she was sinking in the snow. After several minutes, her fingers and toes were numb, and Hunter's scowl had deepened to one of the fiercest expressions to ever cross his face.

"That's enough for now. We need to get back inside." She grabbed his hand. His gloves were soaked —just like hers. From the looks of it, his pant legs were too. "We need to get out of these wet things and put on extra layers."

He slowly flexed his fingers. "We can put the dress bags across the side and front windows and tuck them behind the seat belt holders to keep them in place. That'll provide some insulation. We can hang the tux bags across the back window."

"Good idea." She tugged open the side door and crawled inside. With the dresses out of the way, they'd have room to roll out the sleeping bag.

They worked in silence. Hunter secured the garment bags, and Kira sent out the texts and then pulled out more warm clothes for them both. She tossed her boots on the floor of the front seat and waited for Hunter to do the same.

The bags and the snow covering the windshield created a cocoon of privacy. She turned on a flashlight to brighten the darkened space. Wiggling out of her wet jeans took effort with the fabric clinging to her skin. She slid on wool leggings, thick wool socks, and an extra sweater. All the while, her attention was focused on Hunter and his struggle to get out of his jeans.

"Let me help." She reached for the waistband, but he didn't relinquish his grip.

"I've got it." His voice was as heavy as the lines of stress deepening on his face. She recognized that look and that tone, gruff, agonized, and clearly not wanting pity.

She sat back on her heels and stared at him in the darkened space. "What's going on with you? Every time I offer help, you're refusing it."

Hunter grunted and shrugged and resumed tugging on the damp material, wincing and muttering expletives the entire time.

Kira's gaze drew, as it always did, to the four dimpled scars on his thighs. He caught her gaze and scowled and finally yanked the material free of his legs. The pained expression stayed as he eased on a pair of sweatpants. Sighing, she tossed him a pair of socks. "I'm tired of arguing with you about this. I don't want to spend the next fifty years fighting with your stubbornness. Seeing you in pain makes me want to help. You know I like helping you, so I don't see why you have a problem with it."

Hunter rubbed his hands over his face. "Kira. Please. Lay off for a while, okay?"

The exhaustion in Hunter's voice echoed that in her soul. Maybe laying off for a while was a good thing. They both were stressed and annoyed. Continuing the conversation would only lead to a fight. But she couldn't resist making her case one last time. "I'm just trying to help you."

"If you wanted to help me, we would have flown." He ground out the words while he winced and tugged on a second pair of sweats.

Hurt and guilt and surprise twisted into an ache in her chest. "What?"

"A three-hour temperature-controlled flight where I could have walked around a bit would've been a hell of a lot better than a ten, no, make that a sixteen-hour drive cramped into a car that is already turning into an ice box. And definitely better than being stuck on the side of the road in my version of hell for the next twelve to fifteen hours."

"I'm sorry." The guilt worsened. She should have realized that... But then anger kicked in. "You should have said something when I suggested we drive."

"You didn't suggest it. You presented it as a here's-what-we're-doing. And then you offered to take every-one's dresses and tuxes. What the hell was I supposed to say then—that we can't because I need special treat-ment?" Bitterness and anger laced his words, icing them even colder in the frosty air. "Making sure your dress arrived safely meant more to you than I do."

"That's not fair."

"No? Well, the situation isn't so fair to me right now either."

Tension hung between them like a thick curtain.

The problem with arguing in a confined, tiny space

was the inability to get away and gain some breathing room. At least the darkness provided a sort of barrier.

Kira wrapped a blanket around her body and then slid against the far side of the two-person sleeping bag. "Great, so you think I'm a selfish person with screwed up values. And I think you're stubborn and impossible. Maybe we should be rethinking whether we want to say those vows tomorrow at all."

The look he sent her was unreadable. He grabbed the second blanket, draped it over his legs, and pulled the sleeping bag's cover over the blanket. "Maybe you're right."

They were as far apart as the bag would allow, and the empty space between them echoed the hollowness Kira felt in her stomach.

With a pained groan, Hunter rolled away to face the side window covered by one of the bags. Kira did the same. She lay on her side, staring at the bag containing her dress, as tears slipped down her cheeks as silent as the falling snow.

# CHAPTER THREE

## SKYE

Two days with her parents were enough to remind Skye of why she'd moved away from home in the first place. She smoothed her hair carefully over the left side of her face and tried to pay attention to the hotel's events coordinator, but her concentration was centered on the conversation her mom held several feet away with three of Aidan's relatives.

"...I can't believe this weather. This wouldn't have happened if she'd gotten married back home. Who would've thought, a snowstorm in March? Hasn't my poor baby been through enough?"

Cringing, Skye tugged on her sweater sleeve and collar as Aidan's relatives—maybe an uncle, aunt, and a cousin—turned to look at her. Heat flooded her cheeks, and she locked her gaze on the two centerpieces the coordinator had placed in front of her. What was she supposed to be doing, again? And where was Aidan? He was late and hadn't sent a text.

The coordinator, Jackie, gave her an understanding smile. "So, if the florist can't make it here tomorrow because of the storm, we have enough in stock to use either the glass bowls filled with shells or the driftwood wreaths wrapped in ribbon with a candle in the middle." She lit the wide pillar candle and then stepped back. "Which do you like better?"

Her mom came over and inspected the centerpieces from all angles. "I like the candles."

"Uh..." Skye still wasn't a fan of flames, but at least she wasn't jumping away from them anymore. "I'm not sure about them, and I don't really like the driftwood."

Her mother's lips pinched. "I don't want you to settle. You were supposed to have roses for the center-pieces. I'm not happy about sloppy, last-minute substi-tutions."

Skye's ears burned and she couldn't bring herself to look at Jackie. A cocktail of anxiety and resentment flooded her veins. She wanted to get away as fast as possible. "Mom, please. These are fine. I appreciate how much Jackie is doing to help us. The storm caught all of us by surprise."

Mom nodded at Jackie. "I apologize. I only want the best for my daughter. She's been through so much since that fi—"

"Mom," Skye cut her off as fast as she could. Jackie didn't need to hear the story about the fire. Before she could say anything else, her dad came into the room and motioned for her mom to join him.

"Sorry to interrupt, but Terri and the kids are on the

phone and the kids are insisting they get to talk to their grandmother."

Her mother looked torn between staying and going, but then she nodded and laid a hand on Skye's arm. "Excuse me, please. I haven't talked to my grandkids in a few days."

"Tell Terri I said hello and I hope she can make it here tomorrow." Skye missed her sister. Smart, protective, and always Skye's defender when it came to their parents, Terri was stuck in Miami thanks to a canceled flight.

"I will," her mother promised as she walked away.

Skye breathed a sigh of relief as her mom left the room, then turned to Jackie. "I'm sorry about my mom."

Jackie waved the worry away. "Not a problem. I deal with nervous mothers-of-the-bride all the time." Then her gaze swept over Skye's shoulder. "And here's the groom to be."

"Sorry I'm late." Aidan's strong hand touched Skye's waist. "I finally got through to Hunter. He and Kira are stuck on a section of highway that's been shut down. They probably won't get here until sometime tomorrow."

"That's awful. From her last text, I know it's freezing where they are, and all the snow…"

"Don't look so worried," he said, even though his gaze looked as troubled as she felt. "Hunter and Kira have lots of food, water, blankets, and their sleeping bag. They should be okay until help can arrive."

"Then why do you look so worried too?"

His brows drew together and he rubbed the scruff on his chin. "Because bad things can happen, no matter how prepared you are."

"What about Emily and Damon?" She turned toward Jackie to update her on the last couple. "Their flight was rerouted because of the storm."

Aidan ran his hand through his hair, mussing the short, dark strands. "They're stuck in Baltimore but are at least in a hotel. Once the roads are open tomorrow, they'll have to drive the rest of the way."

Which meant neither couple would be at the rehearsal or the dinner. Which meant all attention would be on Aidan and her. Mostly her.

Her stomach ached with the desire to get away. And at that moment, exactly how much she relied on her friends became crystal clear. That she had them at all amazed her. For so long after the fire, she'd hidden away —until she'd met Aidan through her voiceover work for his company and he'd sparked a desire for more. His friends had accepted and included her right from the start, bringing color to her once dreary world.

Jackie made a few notes on her tablet. "Don't worry. Everything will be fine. We'll do the rehearsal tonight as planned and then we'll do a quick run-through tomorrow when the other couples arrive. So, which centerpiece do you like?"

Skye tugged on the ends of her hair. "I like the shells, but I'm not sure what Kira, Emily, or the guys would like better."

Aidan's hand slid across her shoulders until he'd

pulled her against his side. "I say that we go with the shells."

"Okay then. Decision made." But the tension gripping her body didn't go away. His presence usually helped ease her stress, but not this time. Too much was happening.

Jackie snuffed out the candle. "Good choice. Everything else is being handled in-house, so we shouldn't encounter any further problems. I'll see you back here in an hour for the rehearsal." She waved and walked away.

Skye eased out of Aidan's embrace. She wrapped her arms around her middle and wandered to the window. The hotel's observatory sparkled in the snow's reflection. The room's walls and ceiling, almost entirely made of glass, which she'd originally hoped would provide a backdrop of a starlit sky and moonlight sparkling over the water, gave an ominous view of the storm raging outside, battering the coast with a blast of white.

The weather matched the annoyance and anxiety crashing over her soul.

She hoped their friends were okay. More than a year had passed since she'd started doing those voiceovers for Kallis Toys. She loved the story Kira told of how Damon had hired Hunter and Aidan to work at the company, needing the friends that he'd made in his Army days to be a part of his post-service life too, and how Kira and Hunter had fallen in love in the years that followed. When Skye had come along, Aidan had claimed that she'd saved him as much as he'd saved her.

Emily was the latest addition to the Kallis team. Kira had pushed Damon to hire her best friend as his assistant, and she took full credit for the fact that he and Emily had fallen in love.

These people had become her family. They had to be okay.

Shivering, she turned away.

Aidan stood before her, his dark eyes searching her face. "Don't worry. They'll all be okay. And they'll make it here in time."

But what if they didn't?

"Right. Sure. No worries." She pasted a smile on her face. Aidan didn't need to know how upset she was. He had enough on his mind, worrying about their friends, and that members of his family had yet to arrive or report in. "We should check on Chance. We need to bring him down anyway for the walk-through."

A half-smile curved Aidan's lips. "I love that little bow-tie you bought for him to wear." He brushed his hand over her hair. "If you want to stay here, I can go get him."

"No. I'll come too. I need to take a walk, even if it's just a short one with an elevator ride."

Aidan's aunt came up to them, her eyes filled with pity. "Skye, your mom told me about everything you went through. How scary that must have been. I'm so sorry."

"Thank you." She pulled the end of her sweater over her hand to hide the scarring there. Two days of enduring polite conversation about the worst time in her life, with people she'd mostly never met before, was taking its toll. Especially because it was brought on by her mom's comments of *poor Skye* and *my baby's been through so much*. Being the object of sympathy and curious scrutiny was the reason she'd begun hiding in the first place.

Aidan's arm wrapped around her waist and he directed the conversation to the weather and the news of their stranded friends.

Soon, more people gathered around them, and the suffocating feeling that she hadn't experienced in *months* was back. Closing the room in. Crushing her.

"If you'll excuse me, please. I need to get the dog." Body hot, gritting her teeth, she stepped through the crowd, holding her sweater tight around her body as she moved. When she reached the hall, free of people for the moment, she sucked in a deep breath, grateful for the moment of peace.

The fast, heavy tread of footsteps behind her was accompanied by Aidan's voice. "Hey."

She turned toward him. "We need to get the dog. We spent so much time chatting with your relatives, and now we need to hurry."

He captured her hand in his as they walked. "They can't exactly start without us."

"No, but the sooner we get started, the sooner we can get through it." The past two days of dealing with her mom had robbed her of any joy. How awful was it that she wasn't even looking forward to any of the traditions?

"And the sooner we get to tomorrow night." He kissed her temple and then hit the button for the elevator.

"Right."

During the brief ride, he pulled out his phone. "I told Hunter to check in whenever he could, just so we know they're still okay."

"You're really worried. I can see it in your body language."

"Well, yeah. Cold isn't great for him to begin with, but they're dealing with freezing temperatures out there. That sleeping bag and the blankets will help a lot, but there could still be circulation issues. And if the tailpipe gets clogged with snow and they don't know it, and they run the engine, there's carbon monoxide poisoning to worry about."

She laid her hand on his arm. "He's not by himself. He and Kira are smart, and they'll take care of each other."

"I know." He slipped his key card into the slot and opened the door.

Chance ran toward them when they entered their room. Skye crouched to accept the Golden Retriever's excited greeting. Her tension eased the moment the dog licked her hand and jumped up on her legs. Laughing, she stood, watching as Chance gave Aidan an equally enthusiastic welcome.

"Such a good boy. Are you ready to be a star?" Aidan clipped the leash to the dog's collar.

Having Chance with them was a good distraction,

both for the two of them, and also because he captured their guests' attention.

She felt better. Aidan's brooding expression had eased too. They both changed into the clothes they'd brought for the rehearsal. Aidan's dark grey pants complimented his navy blue shirt. Skye wore a light gray dress that had long flowing sleeves and stopped at her knees. With dark tights and boots, the only parts of her body that remained uncovered were her hands and head.

While Aidan played with the dog, she sat at the desk and touched up her makeup and carefully dabbed extra concealer over the scarring on her hand. Her hair was styled, as it had been for days, cascading to hide the scars on the left side of her face. Her hands shook as she worked, and soon she became aware of the silence in the room. She glanced past her reflection in the mirror and saw both Aidan and Chance watching her.

She quickly set her brush down. "I'm ready."

"I'm not." Aidan strode to her, held out a hand, and gently pulled her to standing. He bent his head and stared into her eyes. "I'm sorry that my reinforcements to distract your mother are stranded in different parts of the country. But I'm here. And I will do whatever I can to make sure you're okay."

The threat of tears pricked her eyes. "I love you."

"I love you too. Now let's get this rehearsal and dinner over with, so we can come back here and cuddle with the dog."

"That's the best idea I've heard all day." She blinked back the tears and grasped his hands. "Let's go."

Five minutes later, they entered the observatory. Her mom stood just inside the doorway, pacing like a trapped animal. "Sweetheart, what are we going to *do* if your friends don't make it here with your dress? This wouldn't have happened if you'd gotten married back home."

"It's snowing in Holiday, too."

"I meant Miami."

"Mom, this really isn't helpful right now. And I'm more worried about my friends than about a dress."

"I know, I know. It's just… two years ago, when you were lying in that hospital bed, I didn't think you would even *make* it." Her voice had continued to rise. Sniffing back tears, she pulled out a tissue. "I want your wedding day to be perfect."

All eyes had turned toward them. Since the wedding party was so small, consisting of just the brides and the grooms, all of the guests who'd flown in had been invited to the dinner after the rehearsal. With the travel delays and hiccups, only twenty people sat in seats, staring at her. But that was twenty too many. Skye fought the urge tug on her dress and smooth her hair. "Mom."

"It *will* be perfect." Aidan clasped her hand and grinned. "As long as Skye says *I do* tomorrow, that's all I need."

His happiness touched off her own smile, and she squeezed his hand back. Aidan was absolutely amazing, a tower of strength when all she wanted to do was crumble. How'd she get so damn lucky?

Jackie joined them, holding her tablet. "Mrs. Galen, could you please take your seat? We need to get the rehearsal underway so the staff can start preparing the room for tomorrow."

With the efficiency of a drill sergeant, the coordinator got her mom seated and ran through the specifics of where to walk and how the ceremony would take place.

Aidan kissed Skye's cheek and then walked down the aisle with Chance and took his place next to his uncle, who was serving as the wedding officiant.

Skye dug her nails into her palms as the guests' focus shifted back to her. Keeping her gaze on Aidan, she walked down the aisle. When she reached them, Chance leaned into her, rubbing his head against her leg.

His uncle smiled at them. "So, tomorrow I'll welcome everyone and talk a little bit about the wedding, and then we'll do the vows in the order you wanted, with Kira and Hunter going first, then Damon and Emily, and then you two."

"Sounds good. You have the vows we picked, right?" Aidan rubbed Chance's head as he spoke. "I have a copy if you need it."

"Got 'em." He pulled a paper out of his pocket and unfolded it. "I can't believe you all wrote your own vows."

Skye glanced at Aidan and smiled. "Not much about this wedding is traditional, so we figured the vows shouldn't be either."

"Fine by me. I always enjoy when people put their own spin on it." He put the paper away. "And you have your rings?"

"We're all set there." Aidan nodded. They'd picked up the matching silver bands a few weeks earlier.

"Then, that's it. You'll exchange rings, I'll pronounce you as husband and wife, and then we celebrate."

Jackie came over. "We'll have the cocktail hour at the bar downstairs while we reset the room for the reception. But you'll have space right here where you can have your photos taken while that happens."

"Thank you." Skye grabbed Aidan's arm when Chance leaned more heavily into her legs nearly knocked her off balance. Tail wagging, he licked her hand and then pounced on Aidan. Her fiancé's laughter rang out, rich and strong, then he gently pushed the dog down.

"We'd better feed him."

They detoured to their room to take care of the dog and then headed to the dinner in the hotel's restaurant. Laughter and conversations flowed throughout the room, but the concern over the missing members of their group was the main topic. She and Aidan stopped to speak with Kira and Damon's parents, Stan and Nadia.

"Any news?" Skye almost didn't want to ask, in case there hadn't been.

Nadia's smile was strained. "I received a text from Kira about an hour ago. She said they're still okay. It's cold, but they're as bundled up as they can be. The rescue crews are likely still several hours from reaching them."

She hugged the older woman. "They'll be okay. They have to be."

"I keep telling myself that." Pulling back, she patted Skye's hand. "You two better sit down. I see the food coming out."

After they had been seated, Aidan's dad raised his glass and offered a toast. Skye had met Aidan's parents and brothers on a quick trip in late January. While she'd been nervous about making a good impression, they'd been friendly and welcoming. And the visit lacked the suffocating, hovering concern that marked her visits with her own family.

Sipping her wine, she tried to relax. Damon's mother made a toast next, and the heartfelt words warmed Skye to the core.

But then her mom stood unsteadily and raised a glass. "We miss having our daughter at home, but we're happy she found Aidan. Not every man would be able to look past her scars…"

"Oh no." An icy mix of shock and dread coated her skin. Skye gripped her glass with nerveless fingers. "This can't be happening."

"As some of you know," her mother continued, "Skye was burned at a bonfire at a beach a few years ago. The fire got out of control, and she fell victim to it.

I'll never forget how scared I was when I received the call that she was in the hospital. Or the first time I saw her with the burns on her face and body." Her voice broke, and she shook her head and pressed her lips together. "But Aidan loves her in spite of them."

The roaring of blood in her ears drowned out her mother's words. She hated having attention on herself, she couldn't sit there for another moment, reliving those horrible, pain-filled weeks all over again, or the stares pinging between her and her mother from people who probably shared Skye's discomfort over the toast-turned-speech.

Needing to stop the words from flowing, she pushed her chair back, but Aidan's chair had already shot out behind him, skidding over the floor.

Eyes hot and angry, he tapped his water glass with his knife, drawing everyone's attention and drowning out her mother's voice. "Thank you, Charlotte, for the speech."

Weaving in her spot, her mom gaped at him. "But I'm not finished."

"It's obvious how much you and Dave love your daughter. Skye is beautiful and kind, and I'm so glad she said yes to me. Damon, Hunter, and I have been close for years. I never thought I'd find someone who would understand and accept me as much as they do. But then I found Skye. She loves all of me, and I love her for *all* of her, every single part."

Her mom slowly sank into her chair, aided by Skye's father. She set her empty glass down and then raised another filled cup to her lips with an unsteady hand. Skye's dad attempted to take the wine away, her mother batted at his hand, and they both glared at each other.

Then Aidan continued speaking, his voice as calm as always. And his hand curled over Skye's shoulder, steady and strong. "Everyone, Skye and I want to thank you for coming here to help us celebrate our wedding. We're hoping that Kira and Hunter and Damon and Emily all arrive safely tomorrow, along with the rest of our guests who were affected by the weather. So, thanks again and please enjoy the rest of your meal."

He sat, and his hand slid to the back of her neck. Massaging her tight muscles, he kissed her temple and then leaned in close enough for her to see the concern in his gaze. "Are you okay?"

Her hands—hidden beneath the white tablecloth—curled into fists and she squeezed until her nails bit into her palms. "Sure."

"I'm sorry I didn't get up sooner. I thought your dad was going to intervene."

"I think he was too stunned to move." Telling herself to relax didn't help. She couldn't guarantee that her mom wouldn't stand up again and continue her speech.

For the rest of the meal, she pushed her food around her plate. Frustrated and embarrassed and angry, and desperately trying not to let it show.

Finally, it ended.

Her mom definitely had too much to drink. After wishing everyone a goodnight, Skye and Aidan helped her dad guide her mom to their room. Mom was weepy again, more than she'd been earlier in the evening, and loud. All Skye wanted was some peace.

Aidan tucked his hands into his pockets as they walked away from her parents' room. His body was one long line of tension. "I thought I'd hit the gym. Go for a run. What do you say?"

Skye tugged her sweater sleeves over her hands. "Go ahead. I'm beat. I think I'll go to bed."

"Are you sure? I can stay. Or you could join me."

"Please, go. I'll hang out with Chance." Forcing a smile was harder, but she managed and kept it on until they returned to their room.

"I won't be long." After a quick change of clothes, he kissed her and headed out.

She collapsed on the bed and patted the mattress until Chance snuggled in by her side. Sending a rambling, venting text to Emily and Kira helped, but her stress level was still in the stratosphere.

One more day.

She just had to get through one more day of her mother's dramatics.

But at that moment, she didn't know if she could bear being in the hotel for another twenty-four hours.

No matter how much she loved Aidan.

# CHAPTER FOUR

## EMILY

Emily stared out the window, watching the snow steadily fall from the darkening sky. Baltimore wasn't Virginia Beach, but for now, she'd take the quiet of the impersonal hotel room after the stressful, crazy day of travel she and Damon had endured.

As excited as she was for her wedding, she wanted to be home. Home, where she could better process the secret that she'd been carrying around for the past few days.

So much had changed in the short months since she'd begun working for Damon, and then dating him, and then getting engaged to him and planning the wedding, and more changes were coming.

Pressing a hand on her abdomen, she fought the wave of nausea and nerves. What was the best way to tell Damon? Sure, they'd talked about wanting kids someday. But someday had sounded like a far-off date. After they'd had a chance to get a handle on the whole being-husband-and-wife thing. Maybe in a few years.

Not *now*.

But ready or not, and in her case, *not*, a baby was on the way.

And her family's jokes that she and Damon had rushed the wedding because of a pregnancy suddenly weren't so funny anymore.

Frenetic energy filled her limbs, and she paced the length of the room, but she couldn't outrun her thoughts. Should she wait until after the wedding to tell him? He'd been under so much stress lately with getting the toy company's latest product on the market.

The toy's launch had been the reason they'd delayed their flight. He'd been working around the clock in preparation and hadn't wanted to leave until every last detail had been handled and the first reports rolling in had confirmed the walking-talking teddy bear's success.

He'd been so distracted, first with the toy, and then with their rerouted flight and the drive to Baltimore, she didn't think he'd noticed that she'd been a mess lately.

Shaking her head, she glanced around the room. At least they weren't stuck on the side of a highway like Kira and Hunter. She didn't know how she'd handle dealing with the news and then worrying about being stuck in the middle of nowhere. The rental car they'd had to pick up at the airport wasn't equipped with any of the items needed for snowbound survival.

As it was, she'd barely gotten through dinner. Distracted by her thoughts, she'd dropped both her fork and her water glass, and the tension clawing through her veins had decimated her appetite.

Damon had slipped out a while ago, saying he'd be back with a surprise.

It was a safe bet to assume her surprise would be bigger.

She turned as the door opened. Damon entered, holding a tray with a bottle of wine, two glasses, and a plate of chocolate-covered strawberries. He nudged the door closed with his foot. "I thought this would help us relax."

Wine? She couldn't drink wine. Not now. She tucked her hair behind her ear and forced a smile. "Looks good."

"Then come here and have some." He winked and set the tray on the bed.

Her stomach fluttered with a combination of nerves and needs. Her limbs felt rooted to the spot by the window. They didn't keep secrets from each other.

Damon was rough and tough, yet sweet and kind. The brown hair falling across his forehead, the brown eyes that seemed to see into her soul, and the dimple that flashed when he smiled—would their baby look like him? Or more like her? Would the child want to play hockey like Damon or bake cookies with her during the holidays?

His eyes narrowed. "What's wrong?"

"Wrong?" The question rasped from her dry throat.

"You're staring at me like you've seen a ghost."

"No, no. Things are good."

"You're pale. Your eyes are wide. You look scared. More scared then I've ever seen you." He crossed to her and ran his hands up her arms. The warmth of his fingers seeped through her sweater. "Actually, I don't think I've ever seen you scared before. Sure, nervous, like when we told your parents that we were getting married in Virginia Beach instead of Holiday, but not scared."

His hands were strong and steadying, and the concern on his face was huge. She knew he'd do anything for anyone to fix any problem. He was wired that way. Always focused on making things better. Like his idea for the triple wedding. And like when they'd had that conversation with her parents. They'd emerged from that visit with everyone happy.

But her news would change everything.

He glanced down, and the worry grooves in his face deepened. "You've been playing with your bracelets for days. And you're doing it again right now. So things aren't good. Tell me what's going on."

The two bracelets, one from her grandmother and one from Damon, clicked together on her arm, and she dropped her fingers away from the links. He knew her far too well. She stared at him, debating about dropping the news, how to do it, and whether waiting until after the wedding was better.

He released his hold and stepped back, and then tugged a hand through his hair. "At first, I thought you were stressed about work. I was, too."

She jumped on the distraction. "I'm so glad the teddy bear is a success."

"Me too. But since the new toy is a big hit with consumers, I've relaxed about that. I know I was stressed again with the travel delays and worrying about everyone, but you've been stressed non-stop. You barely said a word during the flight here, and you've been distracted since before we left Holiday. Are you more worried about traveling the rest of the way than you've said? I really think we'll be okay driving tomorrow once the roads are cleared."

"No. It's not that. Well, I mean, of course, I'm worried about us driving tomorrow in case the roads aren't great, and I'm worried about our families and friends arriving safely, and that Kira and Hunter are stuck on the side of a road, and that Skye's mom is making her miserable." She lifted her gaze to his, her stomach fluttering like crazy, and her heart thumping in rapid beats. "But…"

"But what?" Concern grew in his voice and on his features. "That terrified look is back, and I don't like it. We don't hide things from each other. Did I do something? Did something happen? Please, tell me. Whatever it is, we'll fix it."

Wringing her hands together, she took a tentative step toward him. "Maybe you should have some wine first."

Damon pressed his lips together and his features hardened into a stubborn expression. She held her breath as he studied her face. After a long moment, he nodded. "All right."

He walked to the bed, grabbed the laden tray, then brought it over and set it on the desk by her side. The potent worry radiating from him sent a stab of guilt through her. She'd caused that worry. She had to tell him the truth.

She sucked in a breath when he pressed a glass into her hand. Her fingers tightened on the stem, and her mind spun with how to word the news.

He lifted the unopened bottle and showed her the label with a smile. He always went the extra step to make her happy. "I made sure to get your favorite."

Setting her glass on the tray, she pressed a hand to her stomach. "I can't have any."

His eyes narrowed, and his gaze traveled to her middle. "Are you feeling sick? Is that what's going on? Do you need me to go get you something?"

"No. I… I'm…" She offered him a weak smile while her heartbeat thundered and her mouth went dry. "I'm pregnant."

Damon's eyes widened, his jaw slackened, and the bottle of wine hit the floor.

# CHAPTER FIVE

## HUNTER

Hunter lay on his side of the sleeping bag, staring out into the darkness. The foot and a half of space separating him from Kira felt wider than a mile.

He was an idiot. He knew that. But it seemed like that was the default lately.

Every bit of cold, every flake of snow, every stab of pain in his legs, reminded him that he was broken and mocked his former strength. Kira might claim that she didn't mind helping him, hell, that she even enjoyed it. But how could she? Wouldn't she eventually grow tired of it? Tired of waiting, of going slow, of helping him with tasks like he was a kid?

He didn't want to lose her. Didn't want to alienate her the way his behavior after his surgeries and recovery had alienated his family.

That relationship was severed on both sides.

They weren't coming to the wedding.

He shouldn't care. Not when it had been years since

they'd spoken. Not when he had Kira's family to love and accept him as one of their own.

He rolled onto his back and squinted at Kira. Her thick hair spread across her pillow, she still faced away from him, as she had for the past few hours. Swallowing hard, he touched her shoulder. "Are you awake?"

"Yeah." She turned toward him and clicked on the flashlight that lay by her pillow. Even in the shallow light, he could see the hurt in her eyes.

Hurting her was the last thing he wanted to do. Hurting her cut him deeper than any of the physical pain he endured. He rubbed at the ache that swelled in his chest. "I'm sorry."

"Me too. I packed the massager for you. And the heated blanket. When I looked at the directions and how long the drive would be, it didn't seem too bad. But you're right, it's been uncomfortable and long, and now we're stuck here. As carefully as we packed, things could still go wrong. We could die out here, and it would be all my fault." Tears welled in her eyes and then spilled down her cheeks. "I'm sorry."

Her tears always ripped him wide open. Hunter brushed them away with his hands. "Shh. We're not going to die out here."

"We could. I was so worried about my dress, so worried that it would be lost because the airlines *always* lose my luggage, and then our wedding would be ruined. But if something happens to you, like hypothermia, more nerve damage, or something worse, I'd never forgive myself. You know you mean more to me than anything in the world. I wish we'd flown out with Aidan and Skye."

"I want our wedding to be perfect too. What happened here isn't going to ruin that. I'm sorry for what I said. Pain isn't any excuse for doing that." He rolled onto his side, facing her. "You're right about me pushing away your help."

"But *why*? We've been over this before. You promised me that you'd let me in. And you're normally pretty good about it. But lately, you've been nearly as stubborn as you were before we got together."

He pulled the blanket over her shoulder and tucked it more firmly around her. The hooded sleeping bag was rated to keep them warm in close-to-freezing temperatures, but he wasn't taking any chances. Temperatures were below freezing. They needed to stay as warm as possible. "Lately, I've been thinking a lot about the ways I screwed up things."

"What do you mean?"

"Seeing how supportive your entire family was with our new wedding plans made me miss mine. So I sent my parents an invitation. Then I called them two weeks ago when I hadn't heard anything." Restless with reliving the memory, he adjusted his blanket. "Let's just say that they're not ready to forgive the fact that I was a mean bastard five years ago."

"Back then, you were coming to terms with some serious injuries and were in a lot of pain, not to mention the way you received your injuries in that ambush attack was awful and terrifying. They can't see past that?"

"Not yet. Apparently, I'm still an ungrateful ass who should be better at controlling his feelings and actions. I know I was on a lot of pain meds then, and I drank too much on top of that in dealing with my anger, so there are days that are foggy and blacked out in my brain. I don't know all of what I said back then, but whatever it was, apologizing now didn't matter." He shook his head to clear his mom's disapproving voice from his brain. "Maybe it's better that they aren't in our lives."

"Hunter." Kira's face creased in sympathy, and she grasped his hand. "I'm so sorry."

He shrugged. Convincing himself that it didn't matter hadn't worked, and he doubted he could fall Kira into thinking it didn't bother him. "The only link I have left is Liam. His flight was supposed to arrive in the morning. I hope he can get through."

"Your cousin is a good guy. I'm so glad he's coming."

"Yeah. And at least I still have your family. They've treated me better than my own parents ever did."

Kira scooted closer until their bodies were lined up, and then she wrapped her arm around him. "And you will always have me."

He reveled in the feeling of holding her against him. She was so warm and the best thing that ever happened to him. "I don't deserve you."

"Don't start that nonsense again. Your injury doesn't make you any less of a man. You're perfect in my eyes, perfect for me. And I need you too."

"Do you?" He wasn't sure. She was confident and

capable, smart and giving, and the most welcoming person he'd ever met.

"So much." She kissed his jaw, then his chin, then his lips. "How supportive you are, how steady, your strength, your humor. When you're gone, I feel like something is missing. And when you're there, I feel complete."

He slid his hand under her shirt and splayed his fingers across her back. Nothing felt as good as Kira in his arms. He slanted his lips over hers, angling for a deeper taste.

Kira's hand drifted down his side until it reached his first scar on this thigh. His muscles stiffened under her touch, and she lifted her head. "What's wrong? Are you in pain?"

"Together forever is a long time for you to be helping me with things." He spoke slowly, voicing the real fear, the one that had been screaming in his mind for weeks. "What if you eventually get tired of it? Tired of me?"

She stroked her thumb over the dimpled tissue, her caress as soft as her voice. "Hunter. Every time I help you, I get to show you how much I care. It's no different than you massaging a muscle cramp for me after a run, or you taking care of something because I need help. And I hate seeing you in pain, but I love that I'm able to help you, to try to ease it, to share it with you. It's not a chore for me. It's an act of love. Every. Single. Time."

Her words filled a void in his soul. He swallowed against his thickening throat and bit the inside of his cheek until the pricks of tears behind his eyes receded. He could see it in her eyes, the way they warmed whenever she helped him. "I love you."

"I love you too." Her lips teased his with featherlight brushes and then she pulled back until he could clearly see her chocolate-brown eyes. "So, no more pulling away, okay? And, we talk things out?"

Nodding, he threaded his fingers through her hair. "I promise. We're a team."

"That's right." She stroked her hand along his thigh, then higher, teasing over his cock. Her movements grew bolder as he hardened under her hand. "Let me make you feel good."

She was already succeeding. He groaned as desire bled into need. Desperate to give her as much pleasure as he could, he slipped his fingers under her bra and cupped her breast in his hand. "I like the way you think."

Her eyes fluttered closed, and she leaned into his touch. "And I like the way you feel."

Before things went too far, he had to tell her one more time. "I do love you, Kira."

"I know you do." She kissed him again. "Now let's create some heat."

# CHAPTER SIX

## AIDAN

Aidan pounded out another mile, his sneakers hitting hard against the treadmill. The hotel's gym was empty in the late evening hour, but the silence during his workout hadn't eased his thoughts or his anger or given him a clear plan of action. Skye was upset. He needed to fix it. But how?

Throughout dinner, she'd leaned into him almost constantly, angling the left side of her body, using him to help hide her scars.

She hadn't done that in months.

He'd been a preoccupied with the nor'easter, and his family all coming in at different times, and dealing with the hotel staff and wedding preparations, and worrying about Damon and Emily and Hunter and Kira, but even so, he still should have managed to be a better buffer for Skye.

But he hadn't.

Not enough.

Not until her mom had stood up, clearly well on her way to being drunk, and made that speech.

Toweling off his face, he switched to cool down mode. Skye should have come to the gym with him. Running together was something they enjoyed, and the activity might have helped her get rid of some of the frustration caused by her family.

He'd thought that with all the wedding guests and chaos that came with three brides and three grooms, that her mom wouldn't be able to hover over Skye so much. He hadn't anticipated the delays the weather would cause, or that her mother would be so worked up that she'd tell anyone who would listen about Skye's experience. Naturally, after hearing the story, people wanted to express their sympathy to Skye, but the story had gone through retelling and retelling. Two days filled with that as an undercurrent to the already stressful situation, and no wonder Skye was exhausted and in need of peace.

Especially after that insensitive speech.

Aside from a few video chats, his only other experience with her family had been at Thanksgiving. For the few days they'd been in Miami, her mom had fussed over her with what he could tell was concern and good intentions, but Skye had grown quieter and more withdrawn with every reference in words or looks that her scars received. It was as though to her parents—especially her mom—she was Skye the Burn Victim rather than Skye the Person.

Along with her sister Terri, Aidan had done his best to steer the conversations in other directions, and to emphasize Skye's normal activities in her life with him, but it was as though their words fell on deaf ears. He hadn't relaxed at all until they'd set foot on the plane for their return trip to Holiday. It had taken days for Skye to come around.

That experience alone had him thinking up all sorts of ways that his relatives could distract Mrs. Galen during the wedding weekend. But the weather delays had kept the bulk of his reinforcements out of town.

The machine beeped, and Aidan slowed to a stop. Maybe by the time he got back to their room, he'd figure out what to say.

After wiping down the machine, he strode through nearly empty halls. Tension built in his muscles. Their wedding weekend was supposed to be filled with celebration, not unhappiness and drama. His hand closed into a fist around his key card.

Drawing deep breaths, he rolled his shoulders. Skye didn't need to see him stressed out. He flexed the bent card, glad it still worked to unlock his hotel room's door and stepped inside.

Skye was curled up on the bed, hugging the dog. Shoulders slumped and head bent, she ran her hand over Chance's fur. She lifted her head and turned to face Aidan. Identical tracks of tears shined on her cheeks.

"What happened?" The words snapped out of him, and he rushed toward her. Instead of answering, she cuddled the dog closer. Aidan perched on the edge of the mattress. "Baby, talk to me."

She tugged her hair over the scars on her face and

then angled her head to hide that side from him. "I can't do this."

"Can't do what?" Muscles tight, he touched her shoulder. He hated when she felt she needed to hide her scars from him.

As if following his lead, the dog laid a paw on her leg. Chance, not an official therapy dog, had ended up being just that, providing comfort both to him in dealing with his PTSD, and to Skye.

"My mom. Our guests. The stares. The questions. All of it." Skye faced the window again, and her voice grew soft as a whisper. "I wish it was just the two of us here. No one else."

Frustration battled with concern. Why hadn't she told him how she really felt about a shared wedding? Aidan raked his hands through his damp hair and blew out a long sigh. "Is that what you really wanted? If so, you should have said something."

Skye shrugged, then nodded, and then shook her head. "I liked the idea of sharing the spotlight with the girls and not having all the attention on me. And I know how important it was for you to share this experience with Damon and Hunter. But I didn't think it would be this hard."

"Look, I love those guys. But you're my everything. You and your needs come first." He clasped her soft hand in his and rubbed his thumb over the scarred skin.

She stared at their joined hands and shifted until she'd linked their fingers together. "Your needs are as important as mine."

Gratitude for her words washed over him but couldn't drown out his worry. "I appreciate that. But as long as I'm marrying you, I don't care where or how we do it."

Her gaze landed on her engagement ring. "It's a little late to change things now."

"Not if that's what you want. We can go to a court-house tomorrow or ask my uncle to marry us privately tonight or tomorrow or Sunday morning."

"No. That would cause a lot of attention, and I don't want even more drama. Besides, I do want to share the day with Kira and Skye and the guys. They're our family."

"They are."

"It's the rest of my family, mainly my mom, that's the problem."

"I noticed." He pulled her into his arms. She rested her head against his chest and breathed in deep. Holding her close, he rubbed her back. Long moments later, as he continued his caress, her heart calmed its frantic beats and her taunt muscles eased.

"If Terri were here, she'd help run interference. Even my dad isn't bad unless my mom gets him worked up. But my mom…"

"Trying to distract her hasn't work. I'll say some-thing directly to her."

She pulled back until she met his gaze. "No."

He traced his fingers over her cheek. "You need to be comfortable and happy. It's my job to make sure that happens."

Her gaze softened and turned almost shy. "You always make me happy."

Aidan melted inside. No one had ever appreciated him as much as this beautiful woman who'd consented to share his forever. He wrapped his arms around her again, breathing her in while he stared out at the snow falling into the sea. "Good. If you had any idea how much I love you…"

Skye guided his hands to rest over her heart. "I love that you put up with my anxiety and worries and that you love me enough to want to spend our lives together. I don't know why you love me, but I'm happy that you do."

He moved one hand to cup her jaw and slowly brushed his thumb along her cheek. "I couldn't do anything but love you. You're so loving and giving. Your heart is huge. You inspire me every day." When she began to shake her head, he stopped her by bringing his other hand up to frame her face. "You do. And you're exactly what I need too. Your voice, your touch, your presence is a light I count on to see me through the darkness."

"Aidan." Her voice broke on the word and with tears shimmering in her eyes, she pressed a kiss to his palm.

Carefully shifting the dog, he rose and pulled Skye to standing. She watched him, not saying a word, just holding onto his hands like she never wanted to let go.

"Come with me." Maybe a hot soak would help her relax. He drew her into the large bathroom and turned on the tap in the bathtub. Then found bath salts and added them in. Soon, the scent of the sea filled the steamy air. "I know the past couple of days have been tough. I'm sorry I didn't see how exactly tough until tonight."

"I didn't want to say anything because you're already so worried about Hunter and Kira. You didn't need to deal with my family drama."

"But starting tomorrow, they're my family too. Things can't continue as they've been. I can't have what happened at Thanksgiving or what happened these past few days keep happening. Not when it gets you so upset."

Skye bit her lip. "I know I need to talk to her, but I'm not exactly sure how. I know it's coming from a place of love, so I don't want to hurt her."

He cupped her cheek with his hand. She was such a sweet soul. "I'll help you think of a way. I'm proud of you."

"For what?"

"For dealing with all of the questions the way you have. I know you don't like attention, but you've handled it great."

She linked her arms around his neck and pulled him until her lips touched his. "I never thanked you for standing up and getting her to stop at dinner."

"Like I said before, I wish I'd stood up sooner." He leaned back and tugged his shirt over his head.

Her hands followed, sliding along his chest and coming to a stop at the waistband of his shorts. He let her strip him and then reached in the tub and turned off the water. When he turned back, her dress was halfway up her torso. He helped her remove it, and then her tights, and then her bra and underwear.

Smiling shyly, she wrapped her arms around her torso, but he didn't want her to hide. He tugged her hands away and holding her gaze, he stroked his hands over smooth and scarred skin, loving every inch of her. She'd relaxed so much around him, come so far. But every now and again, all that self-consciousness resurfaced. He'd gladly spend the rest of his life doing his damnedest to send it away.

He drew her into the tub and settled behind her in the hot water. The heat eased his muscles, but holding on to Skye eased his soul.

She relaxed against him, her head resting on his shoulder and her hands tracing patterns on his skin. He continued massaging and teasing until her breaths were deep and even and her sighs were from his touch, and her kisses were as passion-filled as his.

They'd helped each other face fears and demons of their pasts. And, together they'd face down whatever else came their way. She was all he needed.

Just Skye. By his side. For always.

## CHAPTER SEVEN

### DAMON

The bottle of wine rolled over the carpet. Damon stared at Emily while his lungs fought to take in air and his mind processed the word. "Pregnant?"

Emily nodded. Biting her lip, she hugged herself. "A little less than two months along."

A baby.

They were having a baby.

Elation and shock overwhelmed him in equal amounts. For once, he was speechless.

"I know we hadn't planned it this way." Her bracelets clinked together as her fingers twisted in the delicate chains. "Say something. Please."

Love swept through him, a strong current that pushed him forward. He brushed Emily's dark hair from her face. "We made a person. *We made a person*," he repeated, louder, and then scooped her up and swung her in a circle before setting her on her feet. "I love you so much."

Sculpted brows rose high on her forehead. "You aren't angry? I know we said we wanted kids someday, but I know we didn't mean this early. Damon, this is *so* early. We haven't even been together a year yet."

"We might not have planned it to happen this way, but I'm so freaking happy. A baby. I can't believe it." Then a thought occurred to him. She wasn't smiling. Not even a little. In fact, she still looked downright terrified. "Are you happy?"

"Since I found out, I was too busy being scared and stunned, and then too worried about how and when to tell you and how you'd react to the news to feel anything else." A smile slowly spread across her face. "But I am happy."

Relieved, he laughed and threaded his hands through her hair, then he leaned in and kissed her. Her mouth, so soft, opened under his. With a groan, he licked inside.

Her hands curled into his sweater even as her head fell back, exposing the long column of her throat. He stroked his fingers along the smooth skin, his body burning with the need for more. More access and more exposed skin, more kisses and more caresses. Harder. Faster. Deeper. He slid his hands under her sweater, claiming every inch in possessive strokes, and groaned as Emily thrust her hips against his cock. He wanted to strip them both and take her hard, against the window, over the desk, against the wall, on the bed, in the shower. His mind spun with scenarios, wicked fantasies that would leave them sated.

But he feared being rough now. Even though the

rational part of his brain knew it was fine, the other side, the what-if side, shouted a reminder about the baby. Gentling his kisses and his strokes along her skin, he eased back until they were feather-light.

Then he fell to his knees. Laying his hands on her hips, he kissed her belly. His thoughts spun. First with joy—that was their kid growing inside, tiny and perfect and waiting to be loved. Then with panic—he knew nothing, absolutely nothing about babies. He had so much to learn. "So, you're due in October?"

"The doctor said late October."

"It would be cool to have a Halloween baby. Think of the great parties we could have for him or her." He retrieved the bottle of thankfully unopened wine from the rug and then stood and set the bottle on the desk. "You scared me. I've never seen you so pale."

"I wasn't sure how you'd take the news."

Now that the shock had worn off a bit, he wanted to know every detail. Pressing a kiss to her palm, he drew her to sit next to him on the bed. "When did you find out?"

"A few days ago, when I went to the doctor to have her confirm it."

"Wait—" He frowned. "Confirm it? So you went to see her, suspecting the pregnancy? Does that mean you had morning sickness? That's literally the only thing I know about pregnancy."

"I started feeling a lot more tired but figured it was due to working all those late nights leading up to the toy launch. But then I realized I skipped a period, so I took a home test, and it was positive."

He gaped at her, annoyed with himself for be so distracted by work that he hadn't noticed anything else. "We're practically living together, and we work together all day long. Why didn't you say anything?"

"Because I know those things can have a false positive." She stroked her hand over his brow. "And I knew how stressed you were about the toy launch, so I figured it was smarter to wait and have the doctor confirm it. I didn't want to worry you for nothing."

He gently grasped her hands in his, sorry that she'd gone through any of this alone. "You could have worried me. You should have. Because it wouldn't have been for nothing. You've been dealing with the worry and I could've been sharing that with you, and maybe helping you worry less. Or taking the worry away completely because I wouldn't be anything but happy about the fact that we made a kid."

Emily smiled and kissed him. "I appreciate that. I didn't say anything because, well... Don't get mad, but sometimes you fly off the handle when you receive news."

He couldn't deny it. She was right. "But only when that news negatively affects people I care about. I'm not a hot-head all of the time."

"I know that's true. But this is big. And it's so soon. I wasn't sure how you'd feel about it."

"Wasn't sure?" He considered her worry while sliding

his arms around her waist and realizing her bullseye accuracy. He pulled her close, nestling her against him. "You came into my life when I wasn't expecting it. And I fell in love with you when I thought I'd never love anyone again. If you look at things that way, it only makes sense that this baby would make a surprise appearance, because the best things in my life have happened that way."

Tears sparkled in her eyes, and she squeezed his hand. "I love you."

"I love you too." He kissed her again, lingering long enough to stoke the fires of desire again. "Our families are going to be thrilled."

"Let's not say anything until after the wedding. I don't want to take away any of the spotlight from Kira and Skye."

His heart warmed at his sensitive, caring bride's thoughtfulness. "Deal."

She rested her head against his shoulder. "I don't know much about babies. And I don't know what I'm supposed to expect now that we're expecting."

"We'll learn together." He wrapped his arms around her and held tight. Happiness spun out, spilling over until he was beaming. "I guess we won't need the condoms I packed."

Emily's shoulders shook with her laughter. "No, I guess not." She pressed her lips to his neck, then his jaw, and her hands slipped into his hair and tugged at the strands.

The spark of desire, always lit, burned into a fire of want and need.

With a growl, he shifted his hands under her sweater. Petal soft skin that he'd never tire of touching met his hand. She sighed into his mouth and urged his hands higher. His fingers sought the swell of her breast, and he hardened when he felt her nipples pebble against his palms.

Easing his lips from hers, he slipped her shirt over her head. His fingers slid over the emerald green silk of her bra. He flicked the straps off her shoulders and managed to get the front-clasp open on the first try. Her breasts spilled into his hands, and he groaned as he closed his mouth over hers once again.

Her hands were busy tugging at his shirt. He broke away long enough to pull it over his head and toss it aside.

Gazing at her stomach, he knelt beside her and opened her jeans and tugged them off. Her white panties covered in tiny green shamrocks made him smile. "You and your seasonal underwear."

"Saint Patrick's Day is next week." She lifted her hips to help him slip them off.

"I am feeling lucky." He stroked his hands over her torso and pressed kisses along her stomach. "I can't believe we're really having a baby."

Emily ran her fingers through his hair. "Me neither."

Pressing against the mattress on either side of her, he pushed forward and into her kiss. Her hands on his shoulders urged him to follow her as she lay down.

He shifted his weight to avoid crushing her, took a second to kick off his jeans and boxers, and then gathered her close, stroking his hand through her hair, along her back, down her center, anywhere he could touch.

Her hands were as restless, grabbing onto his muscles as their legs tangled together and they arched into each other.

Supporting his weight on his forearms, and holding her gaze, he sank inside her, drunk on the knowledge of what they'd created and high off the pleasure pulsing through him.

The need to rush evaporated. They rocked together in a slow, sexy rhythm that increased the feeling at every point of contact—her hands on his back, her lips slanting under his mouth, their torsos brushing with every thrust, and their legs sliding together on the sheets. He waited, determined she hit her peak first, and then ground his hips into hers as he followed her over.

He loved her more than anything.

He couldn't wait to marry her.

She'd given him more than herself.

She'd given him a family.

# CHAPTER EIGHT

## SKYE

T-minus three hours until the wedding.

Excitement swirling in her veins, Skye rushed with Aidan to the hotel lobby. After hours of phone calls and texts, Damon and Emily and Kira and Hunter had finally arrived.

Relief didn't begin to cover the feeling when she saw her friends. Along with various family members, she hugged them and listened to Kira's breathless recounting of being stuck in the snow, and Damon's equally dramatic, and somewhat embellished—thanks to laughing clarifications from Emily—retelling of their rerouted flight, hotel stay, and drive.

Although the siblings competed for the biggest reaction, they hugged each other tight and kept saying how glad they were that the other was safe.

Their events coordinator Jackie emerged in the middle of the celebration. "We have less than three hours until the wedding. I'd suggest that our new arrivals get checked in, and then everyone begin to get ready."

Aidan pulled Skye back. "Before you rush off to get dressed, come back to the room with me for a minute?"

"Sure." She turned to Kira. "We're still getting dressed in your suite, right?"

"Yep. I'll text you the room number."

Skye kept glancing at Aidan as they walked. His long strides ate up the distance, and she had to increase her pace to keep up. Not buying into the notion that it was bad luck for the bride and groom to see each other before their wedding, they'd spent the day together, huddled away from everyone else, after Aidan had issued a firm statement that they not be disturbed. Being with Aidan was her sanctuary. The uninterrupted hours they'd spent together soothed her on multiple levels.

When they reached their room, he handed her the box containing the bow tie she'd purchased for Chance. "I thought you'd want to help me put it on him."

"Of course." Pleased, she crouched next to Aidan and the dog rocketed into their arms. She held him while Aidan attached the tie to Chance's collar. "He looks so cute."

"Just him?" Brows raised, eyes twinkling, Aidan managed to look innocent.

Laughing, Skye kissed his cheek. "Not just him. You, too. And you know it."

He cupped her cheek. "Now that the others are finally here, the focus won't be so concentrated on us. I hope your mom doesn't say anything to upset you while you guys are getting ready."

"Having Kira and Emily and my sister there will help." Her sister Terri had arrived right after brunch, and their mom had been too busy nursing a hangover to discuss anything at all, but both were supposed to come to Kira's room to help Skye with her dress, hair, and makeup. "Not to mention Kira's mom and Emily's mom."

"Still. Call me if you need me." His fingertips stroked her skin. "Chance and I can be there in no time."

She kissed his palm. "My hero."

His features grew serious. "I'll always try to be."

Chance barked and nudged his head in between them, breaking the moment. Grasping her hands, Aidan pulled Skye to her feet. "Did Kira text you yet?"

She snatched her phone off the desk, read Kira's message, and then sent Kira's room number to Terri and her mom. "Yep. So I guess I'll head up now. They're staying on the floor above us."

He held up his own phone. "Chance and I will walk you. Hunter and I are getting ready in Damon's room."

Focusing on Chance and Aidan kept her calm during the short trip to Kira's suite. Aidan's kiss at the door, deep, and long, and followed by a breathless "I can't wait to marry you" made her forget all about worrying over what could go wrong. Her gaze followed him as he walked down the hall.

"Come in, come in," Kira called out, tugging the door open. Behind her, the garment bags hung from a luggage cart, and Nadia, Emily, and Emily's mom all waved. "Now, the dresses might be a little wrinkled because we used them to help insulate the car."

Emily radiated a glow, happiness beaming out of her face as she smiled. "I have this picture in my head of you and Hunter huddled together in the car under yards and yards of lace and tulle, trying to keep warm. I'm definitely telling the story that way and not mentioning your sleeping bag or blankets at all."

Kira grinned. "I will totally support your version of the events. Wedding attire to the rescue." Then she turned to Skye. "The front desk clerk said she'd send up a steamer from housekeeping in case we need it."

"I'm sure it's fine. The most important thing is that you and Hunter are okay." Skye opened her bag's zipper. The mermaid-style lace gown was wrinkled but still beautiful. With long sleeves made of lace, collar-bone-skimming neckline, and a body-hugging silhou-ette, it was sexy and yet almost completely covered her scars.

As she removed the dress from the bag, a knock sounded on the door, followed by her sister Terri's voice, calling out, "Happy wedding day, ladies!"

Carrying a cup of coffee, her mom followed Terri into the room. They greeted the others and made their way around luggage and bags to her. "Oh, your dress is beautiful. The pictures you sent didn't do this justice."

Terri nodded and set down her makeup kit. "I love it. It's going to look amazing on you."

Skye hung up the dress and smoothed it as best she

could. Thank goodness the hotel had a steamer. "I'm glad you guys like it."

"Of course, I wish you would have come home and let us go shopping with you." Mom shook her head and sniffed. "I feel like we weren't a part of the wedding planning at all."

Skye bit her lip and forced down her simmering frustration and the temptation to remind her mom of her hijacking of the wedding plans back in January. She didn't want to get into any of that now. "I'm sorry you were hurt by that. With three of us sharing the bride role, the three of us had to make wedding decisions together."

"I understand, but you almost died in that fire, and I thought—"

"Mom." Exasperation released the word in a rush, and it reverberated through the room. Skye tugged her hand through her hair. "Stop. Please. Stop bringing it up all the time."

Her mom looked taken aback. "What do you mean?"

In the corner of Skye's vision, Kira and Emily and their mothers moved toward the door, no doubt giving them privacy. She sucked in a deep breath. Time to have the conversation, whether she was ready or not. "The scars, the burns, and the fire are all you can talk about, and it's making me crazy."

"I can't help it. We could have lost you."

"But you didn't." Her heart softened at the anguish creasing her mom's features. She couldn't fathom the pain her parents had gone through, seeing her so hurt back then. But reliving the hurt wasn't helping anyone heal. "Constantly hearing about it makes me really self-conscious. Especially this weekend, when our guests should be focusing on the wedding, not what happened to me."

"I never thought you'd ever have a wedding." Mom's gaze drifted to somewhere behind Skye, past Terri, toward the dress. "I thought you wouldn't even make it out of the hospital."

"But I did. I was lucky." Lucky that she'd survived and hadn't sustained worse injuries. Lucky that she'd had a family to care for her. Lucky that she'd found Aidan to love her. "But when all you do is remind me of what happened, it's like you stopped seeing me that day. Like I've become nothing more than these scars. That I'm no longer the daughter who shares your love of the beach or the one who used to help you bake during holidays."

A light crossed her mother's features. She set down her coffee. "Maybe I do obsess about it. Terri has told me the same thing." She nodded at Terri, then turned back to Skye. "The last thing I want is for you to be unhappy, or to think that your scars are all I see. They're not. I'm sorry."

For the first time in months, Skye felt most of her anxiety dissipate. Expressing her true feelings freed her more than she could have expected. Now she had room to try and see her mother's perspective. "I love that you care so much. You guys took such good care of me back then. I'm better now, but all of our conversations are still filled with reminders of things I already know that I need to do, like wearing sunscreen and covering up the skin before going out in the sun."

"I can't promise that I'll stop that part. I'm your mom. I can't stop needing to make sure you're okay."

"Maybe we could reduce the reminders to ten-percent of our talks instead of ninety?" She offered the suggestion with a smile. "Don't forget, I have Aidan now. He always takes care of me."

Her mom's eyes warmed, and she nodded. "I'm glad you found him. He's a good man. Dad and I will try to be better. We'll focus on you, not the scars. I promise."

"Thank you." She hugged her tight. "I love you."

"I love you too. Now, let's get you ready."

# CHAPTER NINE

## KIRA

Waiting for Skye and Emily, Kira stood in the small room off the side of the observatory, wedding dress on, a bouquet of orange roses in hand, and more than ready to say *I do*.

So much had changed in the past twenty-four hours. She and Hunter had gone from stranded in the snow to storm survivors, they'd gotten through their first major argument, *and* they'd made it to the wedding on time.

She peeked into the observatory. The large glass-paned room, decorated in orange, yellow, and white roses, was beautiful. Rose petals were strewn in the aisle, and tulle and ribbon in orange and white adorned the backs of the guests' chairs. The clouds had lifted, and the moon shined bright in the starry sky.

It was as perfect a setting as she'd hoped.

Smiling and waving at members of her family, she felt a pang as she thought about Hunter's parents. Sometimes, things didn't work out with a happy ending, like they did in books and movies. But at least he had his cousin Liam, who'd arrived moments ago. Liam was one of the happiest guys she'd ever met and, more important, he loved Hunter.

Her gaze drew to her husband-to-be. Hunter stood at the far end of the room, so handsome in his dark tux, next to Aidan and Damon. The three of them were deep in conversation, thick as thieves, as always. Aidan's dog sat quietly at their feet.

Her parents came in and hugged her. When her dad pulled away, he smiled at her with tears in his eyes. "Princess, you look beautiful."

"Thanks, Dad. Mom did a good job helping with my hair, didn't she?" She touched a careful hand to the partial up-do. "Is it still okay?"

"It's perfect." Mom brushed a stray strand away. "My baby is getting married." Then she glanced down the aisle at Damon. "Both of my babies."

Kira smiled again at Hunter. "Yeah."

Then, Dad's face grew serious. "I'm so proud of you. Of the woman you've become. Smart and kind and loving. You're all that we could have asked for in a daughter."

Tears pricked her eyes. Kira blinked them back. "I was thinking the same thing about you guys. You've always been amazing, not just to Damon and me, but you opened up our family to include Aidan and Hunter all these years, too. Especially in light of what's happened with Hunter's parents, I want to say thank you. I'm proud to be your daughter."

Dad sniffed and fumbled in his pocket until Mom handed him a tissue. "Now you're going to make us cry."

Mom hugged her again. "Before the waterworks begin, we want to talk to Damon too. We'll see you after the ceremony."

Kira watched them walk to her brother. Most of the guests were settled in the rows of chairs, but a few milled around, visiting with each other. The fact that all of the guests who'd traveled had actually arrived without any accident or injury was just one more reason to be grateful.

Skye and Emily joined her. Her best friends looked beautiful in their gowns. Skye glanced at her reflection in one of the floor-to-ceiling windows and adjusted her veil. "Look at us."

Emily pressed a hand to her stomach. "After the chaos and planning of the past two months, and especially the craziness of the last few days, I can't believe it's finally time to walk down the aisle."

Kira nodded and grinned at their reflections, overwhelmed with love for her friends. "I'm really happy things worked out the way they did, with my original plans getting ruined. Being able to share everything with you guys has been so much better."

Their event coordinator came in, tablet in hand. "Ladies, you look beautiful. We're ready to start now. I'm going to cue the music."

"Thank you." Kira stepped in front. They'd decided she would walk down first.

After the first strains of the violin had played, she stepped into the observatory. All eyes turned to her but her gaze held Hunter's as she glided down the petal-covered path. Strong and kind and such a good man, he was the only one for her. Their time in the car had turned out to be good for their relationship.

He smiled and then winked at her as she took her place on the opposite side of the officiant.

Emily walked down the aisle next. She held her bouquet of white roses and gazed at Damon like he was the only other person in the room. Kira was ecstatic that Damon and Emily were getting married. Her brother had been through relationship hell, so it was only right that he'd found Emily.

Emily took her place on Kira's right side and whispered, "I think Skye's getting nervous. Maybe we should have insisted that you or I walk out last."

The music continued, and Skye's cue came and went.

Kira nudged Emily. "Isn't Jackie back there with her? Do you think something's wrong? Should one of us go and check on her?"

With the shake of his dog tags, Chance darted away from Aidan and raced down the aisle and into the small side room.

"What the—?" Aidan took three steps forward, then stopped and grinned.

Kira's gaze swept to the back of the room. Skye

came out, with Chance by her side. Relieved, Kira relaxed her grip on her bouquet before she ripped it to shreds.

The dog walked next to Skye, pressed as close as he could be. She clutched her bouquet of yellow roses in one hand and rested the other on the dog's head. Her smile quivered when she met Aidan's gaze. He came forward and met her when she reached the front, kissed her cheek, and whispered something that steadied Skye's smile. Then Skye and Chance took their place next to Emily.

Aidan's Uncle Mick, the officiant, stepped forward. "Welcome and thank you for joining us today as we celebrate the marriage of Kira and Hunter, Skye and Aidan, and Emily and Damon. Today is a celebration. A celebration of love, of commitment, of friendship, of family, and of these six people. These couples have chosen each other, chosen people who inspire them and make them smile, who give them a hand to hold when life's path grows rough, and someone who will always be their greatest champion and closest friend. They've also made my job easier by writing their own vows. I'll now ask each couple to exchange vows and rings. Kira and Hunter, please begin."

Kira handed her bouquet to Emily and then took hold of Hunter's hands, feeling his warmth and strength. "Hunter, we were friends first, but I was always drawn to you like my heart recognized yours. In so many ways, we complement each other, like we were meant to be. I vow to always support you and love you, no matter what. And I mean, *no matter what*. Good times and hard times, and everything in between."

Hunter tightened his hold. Warm light shined in his gaze. "Kira, your smile lights up the room, but having you with me lights up my life. You're my partner and my best friend. I vow to always support you and love you, no matter what. Good times and hard times, and everything in between." Then he pulled her closer, and his voice grew deeper. "I promise that I will always let you in. It's because of you that I learned to fully live again."

Behind them, Mick prompted, "And now, the rings."

Hunter reached into his pocket. A strange smile came over his face like he was caught somewhere between too many emotions, then he withdrew the simple wedding band. "This ring was resting against the highest scar on my leg. Its size is almost the same diameter. Sort of fitting, isn't it? Since falling in love with you and being loved by you has helped heal my demons." He captured her hand and slid the ring onto her finger. "Kira, I give you this ring as a symbol of my love. I hope it always reminds you that you hold my heart."

Kira blinked back tears and untied his band from the ribbon around her bouquet. Then she held Hunter's hand and smiled at him as she pushed the ring onto his finger. "Hunter, I give you this ring as a symbol of my love. Every time you see it, I want you to be reminded that you hold my heart. And that, to me, you are perfect."

His throat worked and tears formed in his eyes. Had

she ever seen tears from him before? She couldn't remember. His hand tightened around hers. "I love you, Kira. Always."

"I love you too. Forever." And then she sealed her promise with a kiss.

# CHAPTER TEN

## EMILY

Emily smiled so hard, witnessing the obvious love between Kira and Hunter as they exchanged vows, that her cheeks ached. Her best friend deserved someone as strong and kind as she was herself.

When they stepped off to the side, Mick addressed the crowd. "And now, Emily and Damon."

She handed her bouquet to Skye and walked to meet Damon in the middle of the semi-circle created by their friends.

She was surrounded by old and new, both in friends and family and in what she wore.

Her grandmother's silk and lace gown had been transformed. They'd removed the sleeves, created a heart-shaped neckline, managed to salvage the row of tiny buttons at her back, and added a jeweled belt at the waist. The veil was original. And to keep up with the old, new, borrowed, and blue, she'd borrowed her mom's pearl earrings, and had managed to find blue underwear that spelled out Bride on the back in blue sparkles. She thought Damon would get a kick out of those.

His eyes sparked heat when he grasped her hands in his. Then his gaze darted down to her stomach, and he grinned.

He really was happy.

And so was she.

"Emily," he began, "I never thought I'd find anyone to love me. But you came into my life and made everything better. Made me better. You allow me to be myself, and encourage me and support me, and challenge me to be my best. For these things, I'm grateful. You're generous, caring, sentimental, and sweet. Before the ceremony, my mom told me that you soften my rough edges. You do more than that, you softened my heart. I promise to always love you, support you, and to always be someone you're proud of."

Few men would be brave enough or strong enough to publicly proclaim their deepest feelings. But her man did in a strong, confident voice that made her heart skip and swell. She locked her gaze on his eyes and spoke from the heart. "When I met you, love was the last thing I was looking for, but once I got to know you, I couldn't help but fall. I love how you always take care of the people around you, and that you care so much about everything. I love your passion and work ethic, and that you're someone I can lean on. People may tease that we've rushed into this, but my heart has never been more sure. I love you, Damon. I promise to always love you, support you, and to always be someone you're proud of."

Mick stepped forward. "And now, they'll exchange rings."

Emily loosened Damon's ring from her bouquet. They'd found the matching antique wedding bands at the same shop where he'd purchased her bracelet and engagement ring. Clutching the ring, she faced him.

Emotions raced across Damon's face, and he held her fingers in a gentle grasp as he brought her ring into view. "Emily, I give you this ring as a symbol of my love." He slid the band onto her finger and then lifted her hand to his lips and kissed it.

Her heartbeat increased, ticking in her ear. She held Damon's ring, the metal warm in her palm. With care, she slid it onto his finger. "Damon, I give you this ring as a symbol of my love."

He linked their fingers together and drew her toward him. Her lips parted in anticipation. She wanted nothing more than to kiss him and feel his arms around her. Nothing more than to celebrate all of the happiness. Warm lips closed over hers, and she breathed in Damon's scent and held tight to his shoulders.

Too soon, he eased back. She retrieved her bouquet from Skye and moved with Damon to where Hunter and Kira stood.

The whirlwind romance with Damon, the short time they'd been together didn't matter, no matter how many eyebrows had risen in her family. What did matter was that they'd found each other. And she couldn't wait to see what else was in store.

# CHAPTER ELEVEN

## AIDAN

Aidan felt for the wedding band in his pocket for the tenth time since the ceremony had started. Anticipation pumped into his muscles.

Skye had taken his breath away when she'd walked down the aisle. The dress was both classy and sexy, but Skye herself had never looked more beautiful.

Sure, he'd nearly had a heart attack when Chance had bolted down the aisle. But the dog had a sixth sense when it came to Skye and him. Chance always knew when he was needed. And Skye had needed him then.

Aidan smiled at his uncle as Mick stepped forward one more time. "And now, Aidan and Skye."

Aidan waited for Skye to hand off her bouquet and then linked their fingers together. "Skye, you're the only thing that brings me true peace. I can't imagine life without you, and I don't want to try. You inspire me every day with your strength and your selflessness. I love your soft heart and your gentle spirit." He glanced down at Chance sitting by their feet. "And I love how much you love my dog." His smile deepened as Skye grinned and their guests chuckled. Then he took a breath and gave her his vow. "I promise to always be here for you, to be a place where you find refuge and strength, to love you unconditionally, and I will treasure you always."

Skye squeezed his hand. "Aidan, I never thought I'd find anyone to love me. But then I found you, and you made me want to live again, to take a risk and love again. I love you for your strength, for your calm, for your support, for your friendship, and for your love. I promise to always be here for you, to love you unconditionally, and to give you a place of warmth and peace. I'll treasure you always, too."

Love and gratitude flowing thick in his soul, he pulled out the ring and then paused with it halfway down her finger. "I give you this ring as a symbol of my love, and a promise of my commitment to you."

Skye blinked back tears as he slid the ring home. Something in his chest tightened and then loosened seeing it there. He focused on Chance while Skye untied his ring from her bouquet, and the dog nudged his head into Aidan's leg.

Then Skye grasped Aidan's hand. Her fingers caressed his knuckles, and she pressed her lips together for a moment and then cleared her throat. "Aidan, I give you this ring as a symbol of my love, and a promise of my commitment to you."

The ring slid on, and the unaccustomed weight felt

just right. He ran his thumb over it and then slipped his arms around her waist and pulled her into him. Kissing her now was on a whole other level compared to the very first kiss they'd shared. That he loved her more and more each day was true.

Chance barked twice, and his tail thumped into Aidan's legs. Laughing, he raised his head. "I guess he's vowing to stick by us too."

Their guests' laughter again filled the air.

He patted his side, allowing Chance to jump up but kept the dog away from Skye's dress. No way would he risk anything ripping the lace.

His uncle smiled. "And so, by the power vested in me by the state of Virginia, I now pronounce you husband and wife, and husband and wife, and husband and wife."

Amid cheers, Aidan wrapped his arm around Skye again. "We did it."

On his right side, Damon and Emily embraced, heads bent close together, whispering and smiling. Emily had healed Damon's heart, her care and acceptance had broken through his guards and restored him from a cynic to the friend he'd always known.

On his left side, Hunter twirled Kira, and she spun back to him, laughing. Kira had brought light to Hunter's soul, showing his friend that no matter how he saw himself, in her eyes, he was whole.

Skye's fingers brushed over the back of Aidan's neck, and he smiled down at her. "I love you."

"I love you, too."

Their guests surrounded them in hugs and well-wishes. Aidan hugged his parents and brothers, then Skye's parents, but made sure he stayed close to Skye. She'd sent him a text about her conversation with her mom while he was getting ready. However many times she needed him to shield her or help her, he'd be there, a solid wall of support for the woman who'd given him so much.

Her mom brushed tears away and turned to someone he hadn't met yet, probably one of Emily's relatives. "Isn't my daughter beautiful? And did you know she's the voice of the Kallis Toys commercials?"

A huge smile bloomed on Skye's face. She stood taller, confident, and so sexy. He couldn't wait until they could escape to their room and celebrate in private.

But for now, they had a party to attend.

# CHAPTER TWELVE

## HUNTER

Married.

Finally.

Hunter walked toward the bar that had been set up in the back of the observatory. Kira and Damon had been waylaid by their family after the photographer had finished taking the pictures of the couples. Apparently, every family member had wanted a photo with Kira and Damon, too.

Emily was experiencing the same thing with her huge family. So were Skye and Aidan.

But not him.

Nope.

He was lucky that he had Kira—his best friend and the love of his life. He was also lucky he had Damon and Aidan—they'd become his brothers. And people did choose their own families when they grew up. Friends became family. He was also lucky that Kira and

Damon's parents and the rest of their family welcomed him so completely.

But still, it was awkward as hell roaming around like an unwanted orphan.

"Hunter." Liam strode from the bar, his wide grin so familiar, holding a drink in one hand and his phone in the other. Pocketing his phone, he shifted his grip on his glass, then gave him a hug. "Congratulations."

"Thanks. I'm glad you were able to come." He hugged his cousin tight. Liam had been the only family member who'd kept visiting him all those years ago, who'd kept in contact during Hunter's darkest moments, who hadn't let him push away. And who'd cheered every victory on his long road back.

"I wouldn't miss it. I'm really happy for you. If anyone deserved a happily-ever-after, it's you. Kira's great."

"Yeah. I lucked out there."

Liam tapped him in the chest. "Hey, she lucked out too. Give yourself some credit."

Laughing, Hunter shook his head. But then Liam stepped closer, and his fun-loving, always-smiling front faded, replaced by the serious side he rarely showed. "You went through hell. And I know you still go through it. But don't let anyone tell you that you don't deserve the happiness that you've found here with your wife and friends and her family."

Hunter stuffed his hands into his pockets. "Been talking to my mom?"

"Hell no." Liam snorted. "My dad mentioned it to

me. I don't know where he heard that you called your parents since he hardly talks to anyone on the... let's just say, *difficult* side of the family. He and my mom send their congratulations, by the way. They gave me a card for you and Kira. I slipped it in with my wedding gift."

"That's really nice of your parents." He'd never been close with Liam's parents, seeing them only a handful of times over the years prior to his time in the service and only once after his first surgery. His mother's issues with family members stretched far beyond just Hunter.

Liam pulled out his phone again. "Take a pic with me?"

"Sure." He leaned in and smiled at the image of his and Liam's heads together on the phone screen. They might be second or third or fourth or however-many-removed cousins it was, but that didn't matter. Liam was like Damon and Aidan. They just clicked. "I'm really glad you're here."

"Like I said, I wouldn't have missed it for anything. You and Kira should come out and visit me. If it's during baseball season, I'll make sure you have awesome seats to a Riptide game." Liam's job portraying Fin the Shark, the mascot of LA's pro baseball team, was well-suited to his highly energetic cousin.

"Taking in a game would be cool. And a trip to LA would be great. It's been a while since I've been back."

Liam clapped him on the shoulder. "It's been too

long. I miss you, cousin. And I want to get to know Kira better too. So you'll come for a visit?"

Spending just the past few minutes with Liam was a powerful reminder of how much he missed his cousin. Hunter nodded and smiled. "I promise."

"Cool. Well, I won't keep you from your bride." He jerked his chin toward the door. Kira stood at the entrance, scanning the room. "Love you, man."

"Love you, too." He waved goodbye to Liam and then made his way to Kira. Not just Kira. Damon and Emily and Aidan and Skye, too. They all moved toward him and met him in the empty space that would serve as the dance floor.

Kira slid her hand down his arm. "The DJ is ready, so we're going to start the first dance."

Instead of making their guests sit through three separate dances and songs, they'd agreed that they preferred to share one. The music started, soft strains of a guitar, and he wrapped his arms around his new wife.

Vaguely aware of the other two couples swaying close by, he held her tight and rested his cheek against her head. "We did it."

"We did." She pulled back to look at him. "You're my best friend, Hunter. No matter what. We can see anything through as long as we do it together."

"I believe it. Thank you for loving me, even when I'm not so lovable."

"You're always lovable—even when you're stubborn."

He stopped moving. "Stubborn? I'm—"

"And I'll never stop." Her hands on the back of his neck urged him down to meet her waiting lips. Kissing Kira would always be one of his favorite things to do.

When the song ended, he and the guys left the dance floor as rehearsed, and Kira, Skye, and Emily's dads came on for the father-daughter dance.

Standing shoulder to shoulder between Damon and Aidan, he watched his beautiful bride while several memories flitted through his mind. Sharing the day, hell, sharing the entire experience with guys he considered his brothers had been unreal. They'd been the first people he'd truly been able to depend on. Not only to keep him safe overseas but in everything else too.

He nudged them both in their sides. Damon raised his brow and then leaned an arm on Hunter's shoulder like he did when they were on the bench at the hockey rink and waiting to see if a shot would turn into a goal. Aidan smiled and mirrored the action on Hunter's other side.

The song ended, and his heart dipped. The mother-son dance was up next, so he'd be benched. Out of nothing less than deep kindness, both Damon and Aidan had suggested dropping the dance with their mothers. But forgoing tradition wasn't fair to their moms, just because his didn't give a shit anymore. Hunter had adamantly insisted they keep it in.

Both guys patted him on the back and took off for the dance floor, leaving him on the sidelines.

He simply smiled and reached for Chance's leash. He and the dog would hang out instead. Kira joined him too, wrapping her arm around his waist. He shook off the pang in his chest at how his mom had disappointed him by not accepting his peace offering. Whether or not his parents ever chose to forgive him, he'd forgiven them, and he wouldn't live a life of bitterness. He had a lot to be grateful for.

Halfway through the song, Nadia and Damon stopped dancing and beckoned him over. Hunter frowned. What was going on?

Kira grinned at him, eyes sparkling like she knew a secret. "Go on."

Damon waved at him again. "Hunter, come here."

Hunter passed Chance's leash to Kira and shuffled forward, aware of all eyes on him. Damon patted him on the back. "Mom and I think it's only right for you to dance with her, too."

"No, it's your dance." Raising his hands, he backed up a step. His confusion increased when Damon's dad Stan joined them.

Nadia reached for Hunter's hand. "Stan and I love you like a son. For as long as we've known you, we've felt like you were a part of our family. Today, it becomes official."

"Welcome to the family, son." Stan clapped him hard on the shoulder, then pulled him into a bear hug.

Hot tears stung the back of his eyes. Shit, he couldn't cry in front of all these people. But he could count on one hand the number of times his dad had hugged him over his thirty plus years. Stan and Nadia hugged him at every holiday and family dinner. Honored, humbled, and overwhelmed to be officially a part of a family who had been more of a family to him than his own, he returned the hug. When he pulled back, he swiped his hands over his eyes. "I don't know how to thank you. You gave me a job and treated me like part of your family right from the beginning. Not only you, but Kira, Damon, and Aidan, too. I don't know what I would have done without all of you."

Nadia's hug was gentle in comparison to Stan's. She smiled at him. "You're a good man, Hunter. Now let's finish the dance so these people can eat some cake."

He nodded and glided her around the dance floor, all the while feeling the grateful grin plastered on his face.

All he ever needed, all he ever wanted, surrounded him in this room. An amazing wife, loyal friends, and more parents than he knew what to do with. Yep, he had it all.

He had love.

# CHAPTER THIRTEEN

## DAMON

The starry sky and moon rippling light over the waves echoed the sense of peace and happiness weaving through Damon's blood.

Holding his wife's hand, he guided her over the plush carpet leading to Kira and Hunter's suite. Two hours after the reception had ended, his ears were still ringing from music and cheers.

Not that he was complaining.

Far from it.

He was flying high. They'd done it. Survived the storm and the wedding and absolutely nothing could break his mood.

Emily held tight to the plate containing the extra pieces of wedding cake they'd snagged from the dessert table. The three-tiered cake had three flavors: triple chocolate for Hunter and Kira, Italian cream cake for Damon and Emily, and red velvet for Skye and Aidan.

Shifting the bottles of champagne and water he

carried in the crook of his arm, he didn't let go of her hand when they reached the door, knocking with his foot. Raised voices, tinged with laughter, penetrated through the door. Unmistakably his friends, along with a cheerful bark from Chance.

Emily squeezed his hand and smiled. "I guess we're a little late."

"That seems to happen a lot with us." He bent his head and kissed her. A stop in their room to change out of their wedding clothes had turned into a lot more once he'd had her soft and warm and in his arms.

The door swung open, and Hunter waved them inside. "Did you get lost on your way from one floor down?"

"Funny." Smirking, Damon shoved the champagne bottle into Hunter's stomach.

"Uh," he grunted. But then his eyes gleamed when he saw the plate. "Oh, cake?" His friend and new brother-in-law recovered fast.

"A piece for each of us." Emily set the plate down on the coffee table before curling up on the small sofa under the window.

Aidan and Skye lounged on the couch against the opposite wall, with Chance lying at their feet. Although the couple had changed into regular clothes, the dog still wore his bow tie.

From her place on the bed, Kira pointed to the bottles of wine and glasses on the desk. "Help yourselves. I think we need to make a toast."

Damon handed Emily her bottle of water and poured champagne for himself. "Anyone else need anything?"

He handed out refills and then settled beside Emily on the couch.

"I'll start." Kira raised her glass and then paused. "Wait. Emily doesn't have any champagne."

Emily lifted her water bottle. "I'm sticking with this tonight."

Damon slid his arm around her. They hadn't discussed when to break the news to their friends. It didn't have to be now. No one would question her if she stuck with water. She often didn't drink more than a glass or two of wine at a time. And he didn't think anyone had paid attention to what she drank at the reception.

But Kira frowned. "You didn't want any champagne when we were doing the whole dress, hair, and makeup thing earlier either. Are you feeling okay?"

Damon laughed. Of course, his sister had noticed.

"Well…" Emily twisted toward Damon, brows raised, eyes sparkling with their secret.

The news was ready to burst out of him. He leaned closer and lowered his voice. "Want to tell them?"

She nodded. "You do it."

He set aside his wine, figuring his grin would give him away. "We're having a baby."

The room erupted in cheers, and their friends leaped to their feet. Kira and Skye hugged Emily, peppering her with questions, while Hunter and Aidan gave him high-fives and back slaps, just like when he scored the game-winning goal for their hockey team. And, just like those on-ice celebrations, they followed it by crowding him in a hug.

Aidan elbowed him. "You work fast."

He grinned. So much had changed in his life since he'd first met them in boot camp all those years ago. Hell, so much had changed within the past few months. And these guys had been there with him through it all: heartaches and headaches, false starts and victories, relationship hell and relationship heaven. They'd saved him as much as he'd helped them over the years. His heart was full of all the good things in his life.

Kira hugged him hard and then punched him lightly in the shoulder. "I can't believe it. You knew all day and didn't say anything?"

"Today was a day for all of us."

"I'm so excited."

"Yeah, kid." He used his nickname for her and grinned when her eyes narrowed. "Me too."

He lifted his arm until Emily rested under it. She hid a yawn behind her hand. "I guess our honeymoon in Tuscany will be more food-oriented than wine-oriented now."

She'd worried about how the pregnancy would affect their honeymoon since her energy levels had been flagging, but he'd told her that didn't care if they ended up staying in their hotel room the entire time. They could always go back again.

"I can't wait to see pictures, even if you are too tired to do anything else, and end up just taking pictures of your meals." Skye sipped her champagne. She was more relaxed when she and Aidan were alone, so they and the dog were spending two weeks in a private cabin in the Virginia Mountains. What Skye didn't know was that it was more of a tricked-out, luxury lakeside home than a tiny, sparse space. Aidan had shown Damon and Hunter pictures of the house, with its indoor pool, fully stocked, gourmet kitchen, library, movie theater, and backyard ice rink and sauna. He couldn't wait to surprise her.

Aidan slipped his arm around her shoulders and spoke to Hunter and Kira, sitting on the edge of the bed. "What time is your flight tomorrow?"

With one hand holding his drink, Hunter massaged his thigh with the other. "We have to be at the airport at ten. I can't wait to get away from the cold."

Kira sighed dreamily and looked at her husband. "Bahamas, here we come. I'm so ready for some sun and sand and tropical drinks." She kissed his cheek and covered his hand with hers. He stopped massaging and flipped his hand over to link their fingers.

Damon rubbed Emily's back when she yawned again. He drew her down on the couch with him, and she rested her head on his shoulder. "Guys, if we're going to make a toast, we might want to jump on it."

Emily reached for her water bottle. "Sorry, guys. I'll hold out as long as I can."

"Okay, a toast." Kira raised her glass. "Here's to us. For all the things we've been through together, up to and including the wedding. I'm so glad Damon had the idea that we all get married together. I love you all, and I can't wait to see what the future holds. As long as we have each other, I know it'll be amazing."

"To us." Damon smiled and clinked glasses with the people he loved most. The most special day of his life would always be intertwined with them. Sharing the celebration had been the right decision.

Together, always, was the best way to go.

———

Thank you so much for reading *Marry Me*! I would appreciate it if you would help others enjoy this book too! Please recommend to others and leave a review.

Up next, Hunter's cousin Liam gets is romance in **Enamored**, part of the Game of Love series.

*A baseball romance double-header! Two stories in one!*

After a Spring Training stunt saddles Liam York with a broken ankle, the League's Best Mascot is forced to share the spotlight with the team's solution: a temporary friend for Fin the Shark. But his new co-worker tests the limits of his control.

Claire Devereux spent years caring for her siblings and is more than ready for some fun. She loves every aspect of being Fin's new friend Fiona and is determined to make the temporary gig permanent.

As romance blooms between their on-field personalities, Liam and Claire give in to their passion off the field too. But curve balls from every direction test whether they're better as a duo or if it's every mascot for him/herself.

Meanwhile...

First baseman Slade MacInnes has a lot of balls in the air. His contract is expiring, he's just found his birth parents, and his agreement to do some work with a children's charity has led him to the very sexy and sweet Savanna Soto.

Savanna works hard granting wishes to kids with life-threatening illnesses, something her sister never lived to experience. Slade's no-fear attitude and adrenaline-junkie adventures make her want to break out of her self-imposed safety bubble and live.

Slade figures he's just the man to help her conquer her fears. Each activity draws them closer together with an attraction that sizzles. But when life pushes their differences to a head, will fear win out or can love save the game?

Find all of the books in the Game of Love series:

https://www.susanscottshelley.com/gameoflove

# ABOUT THE AUTHOR

USA TODAY bestselling author Susan Scott Shelley writes romance with heat and heart that celebrates love without limits. She enjoys watching hockey, training for her next run, reading romance novels, and binging episodes of her favorite British TV shows. Susan lives in Philadelphia with her husband and also works as a professional voice over artist. A city girl who likes being out in nature as often as possible, she has yet to meet a plant she hasn't wanted to take home and she really wants a pet crow.

Visit her website: https://susanscottshelley.com

## ALSO BY SUSAN SCOTT SHELLEY

Philadelphia Power series

Against the Rush, Over the Top, Behind the Mask, From the
First,

Powered by Love (series collection)

The Falling series

Falling Faster

Bliss Bakery series

Sugar Crush, Heart of the Batter

Love & Rugby series

Spiral, Spark, Smolder, Shine, Surprise, Swoon,

Love & Rugby, vol.1, Love & Rugby, vol.2,

Love & Rugby, the Complete Collection

Love & Rugby: Season of Love series

Savor, Seduce, Stay

Love & Rugby: Season of Love, the Complete Collection

Philadelphia Frenzy series

Mad Scramble, Hometown Hero, Team Spirit

### Pride of the Bedlam series

Skating on Chance, Holding on Tight, Scoring Slater,
Playing with Pride (series collection)

### Buffalo Bedlam series

Making His Move, Fighting For More, Taking His Shot,
Playing to Win (series collection)

### Game of Love series

Rekindled, Captivated, Enamored,
Game of Love (series collection)

### Rocked by Love series

Love Notes, Love Song

### Holiday Hearts series

Kiss Me Again, More Than Words, All I Want, Marry Me,
Holiday Hearts (series collection)

### Other Novellas

Flirting on Ice, Simmering Ice, Tackled by the Girl Next Door

Sign up for Susan's newsletter:

https://www.susanscottsshelley.com/newsletter